I've Found Her Part 2

I'll Never Lose Her Again

Joy Mullett

To my Beta readers, Lizzy, Amy and Beki. Thank you for your honesty and encouragement.

To my Christopher and Archie, you are my world.

To my parents, who make me feel like I can achieve anything in the world.

Love you forever.

Joy xxx

Contents

Note from the Author

This series contains content that may disturb some readers.

It is intended for readers 18+

The story contains sex scenes, graphic details of violence and discussions of certain topics which some may find triggering.

For sensitive readers, read at your discretion.

Chapter 1

Chloe.

For goodness sake! I am going to be so late. A great best friend I am. I will end up arriving just as Bella and Damien do, spoiling the surprise for Damien. Truth be told, I don't actually think the party will be much of a surprise. Not much gets past Damien. He is probably just going along with it all to please Bella. He's a good one. He looks after her and makes her happy which in turn makes me happy.

I don't usually work on a Saturday, but seeing as I am new to my job role, I felt I couldn't say no when my manager asked me to cover a shift.

I have just moved to London and started working at a youth centre as a counsellor. The session needing to be covered is an information, advice, and guidance session around drug supply and use. Most of the young people attending do so as part of a rehabilitation order. Needless to say, the majority don't actually want to be here.

It was all going smoothly until an argument broke out with a group of boys. "You're a F**king grass!" A largely built 16-year-old screams into another's face. "Lads! Calm down or get out of my session!" They hear me, pause for a moment, but then carry on. They become even more aggressive, and a couple of others join in. Trying to push them apart I get hit and thrown about, caught in the brawl. I have a radio, so I push the SOS button, but no one arrives. Typical. I have no choice, but to leave the room and go and find some help. I get to the staff room to find Jason and Paul sitting watching the football. "Did you not hear my SOS on the radio?!"

"Yeah, but we thought you sat on it by mistake." Idiots these men.

"Well, no actually, I have a full-on brawl happening in my session and I need both of you right now." We all quickly make our way down the corridor towards my room. We are metres away from the door and I realise it seems extremely quiet. I hear a man's voice that I don't recognise. The door is now closed. We all look through the narrow window in the door. All my group are stood huddled together, apart from 4 of them. The 4 who were fighting when I left are lined up. There's a man who does not work here with his back to the door. The man is talking quietly, but I can hear anger and aggression in his voice. The group looks scared. The man turns slightly, and I see why. He's holding a gun at them. "Call the police. Quick." I whisper, Paul quietly runs back to the staffroom. "What the hell do we do Jason?" We both duck down as the gunman starts to move.

"Let's go back to the staff room and wait for the police" Seriously, he's such a wimp.

"I'm not leaving the kids Jason." I try and think of

a plan. I run different scenarios through my head. Shall I go in there and tell him to get out? Shall I bang on the door and then run off? Shall I tell him we've rung the police? All these options don't seem that great and they have a high chance of me, or someone else getting shot. I lift my head up to take another look. He's still walking around the room. I decide I'll get my phone out and video him. If I can't help, at least I will have some evidence. Jason is twitching about, sitting on the floor biting his nails. He's making me more nervous. "Jason why don't you go and see how Paul is getting on ringing the police."

"Alright yeah." He gets up and scuttles off. I hope I never need to rely on one of those two for help. The gun man's voice is getting louder, and angrier. I can hear the kids trying to control their fear, but unable to hold in their screams whenever the guy raises his voice even more, or makes a sudden movement. I am wracking my brain trying to think of how I can help and get this man away from them. I hear the sirens in the distance. At last.

Hopefully this will now deter him.

No such luck.

There's humour in his voice. Maybe he is calming down.

*BANG *BANG *BANG. Oh god no.

The screams are harrowing.

I peek through the window. The man is now making his way to the door. The door I am hiding behind. I look around for somewhere to hide. There's a cleaning cupboard opposite. On all fours I quickly make my way across the hall. I shut the door just as I hear the other one open. I hide there and watch him leave through the gaps in the door. I get a good look at his face. Pure evil.

As soon as he's gone, I run to the front door and lock it, I then go to my group. I try not to be affected by the blood bath of a scene in front me.

"He's gone, help is on its way, everything is going to be ok." There are cries of relief and panic as they realise what has just happened. My stomach is in knots as I realise one of the boys, Tyler, is lay on the floor extremely still, another 2 of the boys are rolling around in a pool of blood.

"Someone go grab as many coats, cloths and towels as you can. Anything to stop the bleeding." A few of them return with clothing garments.

"I need help wrapping the boy's legs, and then we will all go into the games room." I need to get everyone out of this room.

"I did Jason's first aid course last week so I can help."

"Me too" say a couple of the kids.

"Great, come help me. The rest of you go to the games room."

Two of the boys have gunshot wounds to their legs. We wrap them up as best we can to stop the bleeding. They're in agony. We carry them out and get them settled on the sofas. "But Chloe, what about Tyler?" Leaving Tyler lying on that floor is the hardest thing I have ever done. I am no doctor, but I know there is nothing anyone can do for him. He wasn't shot in the leg.

"I'm sorry hun. There's nothing we can do for him now."

I get everyone settled just as the police arrive. One of the cops starts firing questions at me. I am trying to console heartbroken teenagers who have just been hit by the realisation of what they have witnessed. "I don't know his name, and I have never seen him before." Seriously does he need to ask me questions now? "Can I speak to you later, I really need to help these kids."

"And you are?" says the arrogant cop.

"Busy!" I shout to him as I turn and catch one of the girls who has just passed out.

"Miss, I haven't finished speaking to you yet."

"You heard the lady! She's busy!" Bellows the deep gruff voice that makes my stomach flip and blood rush around my body. Josh. Thank goodness. I turn and give him a little smile in relief. He nods and quickly takes charge of the situation. The paramedics arrive, followed by parents and carers of the kids. Damien's here now too, organising and delegating. The police continue with their statements.

"Miss Smith, can you give me a description of the man you saw?"

"Yes I can, he has very short shaved hair.......... actually, I can do better than give you a description, I have him on video." With being so busy in the chaos of the situation I forgot that I had filmed the event. I play the video and I am shocked to see I captured all the shootings. Josh is sat next me, he takes my hand and gives it a squeeze.

"I think she's been through enough now officer. We can send you copies of the video and then arrange for any further questions another day. Come on Chloe I am taking you home." Josh stands and pulls me up with him. I can tell the policeman isn't happy about ending the questions there, but he wouldn't dare argue with Josh.

Josh drives me home. I am currently staying with Bella and Damien until I find a place of my own. Their home is out of this world. It was Damien's parents' house until they passed away, now Damien and Bella live there. We drive down the long driveway. The house is surrounded by trees, we seem a world away from the busy London city. I knew moving to London would involve new experiences, but I didn't think I would experience murder and shootings in my first couple of weeks. I have never even seen a gun, before today. We pull up to the steps at the front of the house. Bella is stood waiting at the door. As soon as I exit the car she pulls me into the biggest hug, her eyes are full of tears. "I am so glad you are ok, I wanted to come but Damien wouldn't let me. He rang me and said you were ok though, well, as much as you can be. Oh Chloe, I've been so worried." We go into the front sitting room.

"I'm fine Bella, shocked but fine." Am I fine though? I'm not sure? If Bella had just been through what I have, I would be extremely worried and adamant that she would not be fine. But it all just feels so surreal. I'm worried about the kids. They may be teenagers but they're still kids. I've only known them a couple of weeks, but I've seen them most days and really bonded with some of them. My heart breaks for Tyler. He was a cheeky chappy and always up to no good, but he didn't deserve this. Bella brings me a cup of tea. "Would you like something to eat? Anything you fancy I'll get it for you?"

"No, I'm fine thank you. I couldn't eat anything right now."

"I'll put the tele on then." Bella cuddles up next to me and puts 'Friends' on. It's always been our go-to programme when one of us isn't feeling well, or is upset about something. Usually, I will talk none stop and pull Bella out of whatever mood she is in. Bella doesn't talk much. It's a confidence thing, she worries too much about what to say. I usually wish she would talk more, but not today. Today, in the words of Martin Luther King Jr, 'Silence is golden'. We sit together and watch one of our favourite episodes. It's the one where Joey dresses in all Chandler's clothes "Look at me, I'm Chandler, could I 'be' wearing anymore clothes!" We both say the line out loud. I start to feel a little better, until suddenly thoughts of Tyler and the other kids pop into my head. The episode finishes and Bella suggests going for a swim. The house has its own pool, well full leisure centre, actually it's huge. I've lived here weeks now and visited multiple times previously and still I haven't seen all the rooms. Bella knows that when I am stressed, I like to exercise to release my frustration. We turn off the tele and leave the room, as soon as we do Josh and Damien appear. "Are you girls ok?" Honestly, they are like spies and have a sixth sense when it comes to us I'm sure. Especially Damien with Bella. They've been checking in on us this whole time, I've seen their reflection in the mirror. I'm not used to someone looking after me, especially not a male. "We're going for a swim."

"We will come with you. I fancy a swim." Says Josh. I roll my eyes, he doesn't fancy a swim, he just wants to watch me, make sure I am alright, I suppose. But it's not like I'm going to break into little pieces.

We all swim lengths, not stopping, in worlds of our own. When I notice Bella has climbed out, I join her in the steam room. The door of the steam room has one-way glass. I watch as Josh gets out of the pool. With one swift push of his big muscular arms and shoulders, he's up on his feet and walking over to the jacuzzi. His blue shorts are stuck to him leaving little to the imagination. I sigh a little too loudly, Bella giggles knowing full well I have just been ogling Josh. "So, what's going on with you two then? You both obviously fancy the pants off each other, has anything happened yet?"

"Nope. Josh thinks of me as his little sister or something. I thought something was there at first, but it's more like a weird protective thing. Maybe he feels he needs to look after me, because I'm his best mate's girls - best mate or something, I dunno. But I don't need anyone to look after me, I have done perfectly well looking after myself up to now." Bella just nods, her attention is now on Damien. They are both in the jacuzzi. Damien and Josh are both very attractive men. Damien in an obvious tall dark and handsome way and Josh in a sexy, mysterious way. He can look quite scary at times, but every now and again, his eyes flicker and I get a glimpse of something that makes me feel...... safe? Protected? I'm not sure why I like this feeling, I don't feel unsafe or that I need protection.

I say my good nights and go to my room. I feel exhausted so I get straight into bed. Now I am alone I replay today's events over and over in my head trying to think of a way I could have prevented what had happened. I feel mentally drained, I really need to sleep but my mind will not switch off. When I was younger and I couldn't sleep, my grandma always told me to write my thoughts down and leave them at the side of my bed. Then I could forget about them for now, knowing they'd be there in the morning. This has usually worked for me, but these thoughts I am having tonight, I couldn't bring myself to write down. They are too horrifying to put pen to paper. I am a very strong person, it takes a lot for me to cry. But what those kids and their families are going to go through for the rest of their lives breaks my heart.

After a while, I eventually cry myself to sleep.

I can hear screams and cries of children. Harrowing, petrified sounds nobody should hear let alone make. He's here. The evil man with a gun. I need to save the children, but I can't get to them. I run but I don't move, I shout but no words come out. He grabs me, I punch out but my arm moves in slow motion and has no power. The screaming gets louder, I try and shout for help.

I feel my body rocking and I start to feel calmer. The screams quieten down and the evil man disappears.

I am back in my room. I'm in Josh's arms, being cradled like a baby. He is rocking me gently. "Hey, its ok, its ok Chloe, Josh has got you." He says to me softly. I am panting, completely out of breath. My hair is stuck to my face with sweat. I let myself calm down for a few minutes while I work out whether I am still dreaming. But no, I am actually, in the arms of a handsome hunk, being rocked like a baby. Once I am fully awake, I push out of his arms and scramble up my bed. "What the hell are you doing Josh?!" Josh stands and faces me looking shocked.

"I heard you screaming so I came to check you were ok."

"Well, I am fine thank you, so you can leave now." Josh nods and leaves the room. I put my head in my hands. I am still trembling. I have always dreamt a lot but that was something else. It was so real. I switch my light on and scroll through my phone, trying to take my mind off it. But it's no use. I decide to get up and go to the gym. I feel guilty about the way I reacted to Josh. He looked hurt by my reaction. He was only trying to help me, I will apologise in the morning.

The gym is two floors down. As I go down the bottom few steps I hear music and someone running on the treadmill. "Sorry I didn't realise anyone was down here."

"I was just leaving." Josh says as he stops the machine and grabs his towel.

"You don't need to leave, I wanted to…." But he's gone.

Chapter 2

Josh

What is her problem? I heard Chloe screaming from the kitchen. As soon as I saw her, I knew she was having a nightmare. I know from experience you should not wake someone from a nightmare, but Chloe was thrashing about so much I worried she would hurt herself. I decided to hold and rock her while whispering calming words. This then woke her slowly. When she first woke and her eyes held mine, I thought I had made a breakthrough with her. But obviously not. I am done trying with that girl now. She is so cold and continually pushes me away. I just wish my other body parts thought the same way as my brain. You know when you really want something but it's really bad for you, but you want it anyway? That's Chloe, she is my double-edged sword.

It's 3am, I don't sleep much and tonight will be one of those nights that I don't sleep at all. I decided to stay here at Kingson Manor tonight to keep an eye on Chloe. Much to her annoyance, I am sure. I don't understand why she dislikes me so much. I may as well get some work done seeing as I can't continue my workout. Damien has a good office set up, so I kill a few hours in there going through our new job assignments, matching the King security team to the most suited role. One particular assignment I have taken responsibility over. Chloe. Damien and I both agree it is necessary to have eyes on Chloe for a while, at least until the gunman is behind bars.

I watch the video again that was taken on Chloe's phone. The man had 15 teenagers petrified and begging for their lives. 3 minutes in, he shoots a teenage boy in the leg, then another. The third boy he executes, shooting him between the eyes. The gunman regularly uses a gun and by the remorseless expression on his face, this isn't the first time he has killed someone. As of yet, we don't have an identification. The police want to speak to Chloe tomorrow. Hopefully, they will have made some progress. I check the home security system and see that Chloe is in the kitchen. I assume she didn't go back to bed. I could do with some coffee.

"Hey" Chloe jumps off the bar stool she's sitting on. "Sorry I didn't mean to frighten you"

"I'm not frightened. I've not slept, so my reflexes are more jumpy than usual" Yeah right, she's been affected by the shooting much more than she realises. Not surprisingly really. She puts up this 'I'm a strong independent woman that needs no help from anyone' persona, but she's only human like the rest of us. "Would you like some coffee?"

"I'd love some, thanks Josh" I stand in front of the coffee machine wondering how to switch it on. Damien has always had the most fanciest of gadgets for everything. Don't get me wrong, I enjoy the finer things in life and have been blessed with good fortune, but I'm a simple kind of guy. Give me a kettle and jar of Douwe Egberts instant gold any day. "Move out of the way I'll do it." Chloe nudges me out of the way with her hip. She tuts and shakes her head with a giggle. I sit at the island and watch her use the machine with ease. Chloe chatters on like nothing has happened, but I can see the tension in her shoulders. I'd love to rub them and give her some release. I wouldn't touch her though, I'd get a punch in the nose if I did. I wish she would let me in. I could definitely make her feel better. "How are you feeling Clo?" She gives me a look. Chloe doesn't like being called Clo. I called it her once and she went mental, I call it her more now, just to annoy her. "I'm ok, I just can't stop thinking about those kids. And Tyler. My heart hurts thinking about him." Chloe puts her head in her hands and I automatically go to her to comfort her, I put my hand on her back and gentle rub circles. She doesn't shrug me off which surprises me. "I'm sorry I shouted at you earlier. I was freaked out by my dream and then shocked to find you holding me. I know you were just trying to help me." I nod, not saying anything just yet. Still rubbing her back, I'm surprised by her apology if I'm honest.

"The police want to speak to you tomorrow. I told them to come to the office, is that ok with you?"

"Yes that's fine. Do you think they have caught him?"

"I'm not sure, but I wouldn't get your hopes up. Hopefully, they will have some leads and have made some progress. Damien will bring you in as I've some meetings this morning." As she looks at me I notice her eyes are glazed over. The sparkle in them has disappeared. Chloe is so beautiful. More than she knows. Her fresh face is dotted with little freckles across her nose and cheeks, she looks younger than her years. Olive skin, dark hair, and a body that looks as if it has been sculpted by the finest of sculptors.

We talk for an hour and drink two cups of strong coffee. I then get ready and leave for work, I have meetings this morning and then the police are coming to speak to Chloe.

Sitting at my desk my mind goes to Chloe. I could have easily lost her yesterday. I need to find this gunman. I have just organised a team of the company's best men to work with the police and help find him.

"Josh, Mr Graves is here, shall I send him in?"

"Yeah, send him in." The guy is late, and I hate lateness. If it were someone else, I would have told him I couldn't see him. But Mr Graves is over from New York and I want to know why.

"Mr Graves, please take a seat." He takes a seat and his two 'bodyguards' follow in behind him. I use the term 'bodyguard' loosely, they may be big, but they are idiots. In fact, the only way they would be less productive would be if they were the walls they are currently leaning against. "So? To what do I owe the pleasure? Are you on holiday, or is this a business trip?" Mr Graves has a debt-collecting business which we currently work with. He lives and works in New York, this is where our team supports him. His visit to the UK was not scheduled and I don't like not being kept in the loop. "It's a family matter actually. My son needs some help. I need your expertise in tracking someone down."

I get all the information I need and put Mr Graves in touch with the relevant team. I wrap up the meeting as time is ticking and Chloe and the police will be arriving soon.

Chloe

I am waiting outside Josh's office as his door opens and a man in his 50s walks out with two very large men who look like Lurch from the Addam's family. The very well-dressed, normal looking man does a double-take as he sees me and comes over. "I don't believe we've met, my name is David Graves, and you are?" He puts his hand out to shake mine. Before I do Josh appears by my side, standing in between me and Mr Graves. "This is Chloe, a very good friend of mine." Josh's eyes bore into the side of the mans head. Not that he noticed, his attention was all on me. "A very beautiful name for a very beautiful lady." The man has a strong American accent.

"You think so? I never really liked it. Although it's better than my middle name 'Karen'." The man looks at me with wide eyes and a strange expression. "I have to disagree Chloe, I also think 'Karen' is beautiful." His eyes haven't left mine. Wow you're too old for me mate. This is getting awkward. I can hear Josh's breathing change. He's getting angry. I do like angry Josh though, so I decide to humour Mr Graves a little longer. "It was my mother's name actually. She was very beautiful." Mr Graves doesn't have chance to respond to this, Josh taps him on the shoulder and steers him out.

When Josh returns, he's in a very grumpy mood. I love it when he turns all alpha male.

The police haven't caught the gun man yet. It has only been 24 hours, but I was hoping they would catch him straight away. The more time goes on the further away he could be. They have got some good images from my video, so they are going to release those today. Hopefully someone will recognise him and know where he is. Annoyingly all the kids have said they can't give a description of the gunman and don't want to give evidence. I can't blame them I suppose, they are all scared. I'm meeting Bella for lunch and some retail therapy. Josh insists on giving me a lift. There's something on his mind. His face wears a frown and he's deep in thought. "Have you ever met Mr Graves before Clo?" I roll my eyes. Josh is the only person who calls me Clo. I hate that abbreviation usually, but when Josh says it, I don't mind. It makes me feel like I'm special to him. Weird I know. "No, not that I know of. Why?" Josh nods thinking. "He seemed very interested in you that's all. The company may work with him, but I don't trust him Clo. Just be on your guard if you see him again."

"Ok, no worries."

We are outside the restaurant that I'm meeting Bella in. As I get out Josh calls to me. "I'll come back and pick you up. Just call me when you're ready." laughing to myself I give him a wave. He's not going anywhere. He will be following me and Bella around all day, I know it. He'll keep his distance though, thinking we don't know he's there. Normally I'd confront him about it, but I'm still feeling a little jumpy after yesterday and the police didn't exactly put me at ease this morning.

Bella's stood outside the restaurant, Damien stood beside her. I can hear Bella speaking to Damien, her voice is raised. "Honestly, Damien, I'm fine. See look, Chloe's here now." These men are so protective, but I am glad it's over Bella. She deserves to be looked after. I give Bella a big hug. "You can get lost now big guy. She's safe with me." I give Damien a playful slap to the chest, and we head into the restaurant.

Bella's happily talking to me about the salon, but there's something not right. Bella looks different. Her skin is paler and glowing, her face looks rounder. "Bella?" I interrupt, mid conversation about the new apprentice they've just taken on.

"You're pregnant?!"

"What? How did you?" Bella's shocked expression quickly turns into a big smile, she puts her hands on her cheeks and her eyes fill with tears. I jump out of my seat, pick her up and spin her around kissing her all over her face. "This is amazing news!"

"How did you know?" Bella splutters. "You're my bestie, I can just tell. I've known you my whole life Bella, I have seen you almost every day. I would notice an extra hair on your head." Bella giggles and lets out a relieved sigh. "I haven't even told Damien yet. I had planned to tell him last night after his birthday meal."

"Oh Bella, I'm so sorry I spoiled that for you."

"You did no such thing Chloe Karen, and don't you ever think that. Do you think he will happy?"

"Of course he will. He absolutely adores you Bella. And if he isn't, then we will bring the baby up just you and me." Bella smiles and squeezes my hand.

"Thanks, love you Chloe." The waiter comes over to take our order.

"We will have a bottle of champagne please. We are celebrating!"

"Chloe, I can't drink alcohol."

"Oh yeah, more for me then. And a jug of water for the pregnant one."

"SSSHHHH Chloe! I need to tell Damien before anyone else finds out. Damien will be so upset if he finds out he's not the first to know."

I am so happy for Bella and what the future holds

for us all. I'm going to be Aunty Chloe.

I'm an only child and so is Bella, we have always been very close, she's the sister I never had, and the closest thing to family I have left now. I was brought up by my grandma, my mum passed away when I was a baby.

We have a lovely afternoon, eating and drinking, well I am the only one doing the drinking. "Tell me Chloe, what is going on with you and Josh?"

"Oh I don't know. He's so grumpy. But so dam hot! Sometimes I think I catch him looking at me like he wants to devour me. But most of the time he looks grumpy and disappointed in me. I'm not sure where I stand. I'm all for making the first move if he's into me, but I don't want to make a fool of myself."

"He's so into you Chloe, I can't believe you don't see it. But you like him though yeah?"

"Like him? Understatement of the century Bella. Every time I see him, I want to rip his clothes off, cover him in Nutella and lick it off!!" Bella laughs out loud.

"You and Nutella. I don't get why you like it so much."

"It's the best, that and cookie dough ice cream. Yeah, I want to cover Josh in Nutella, lick it off and then ride him while eating cookie dough ice cream. Nutella, ice cream and Josh. Heaven!" We both giggle until my belly and face hurt from laughing so much.

"Promise me you won't tell Damien though. He

will be so angry with me. I will tell him when the time is right."

"Oh course." We finish our drinks and pay the bill.

"Oh-oh, the boys are here, and they don't look impressed." I turn and see Damien marching in with his usual scowl and Josh looking half angry half amused.

Josh

I am sat in the car outside the restaurant waiting for Chloe when there's a tap at my window. Its Damien. "Hey, I could have brought Bella home too you know."

"I know, I just wanted to take her out somewhere and I was going past anyway. Have they been in there all afternoon?"

"Yep, 4 and a half hours." Damien gets in the car. We catch up with work for 10 minutes or so until someone entering the restaurant catches our attention. "Is that Mr Graves?"

"Sure is. What the hell is he up to?" The restaurant is getting busy now and there are people blocking our view of the girls through the window. "Maybe we should go in?"

"Not so fast, Bella's been going on at me enough for spying on her. I have an idea." Damien gets out his phone.

"I put the 'Find my kids' app on Bella's Phone. She knows it has a tracker on there, but what she doesn't know about is this little feature." Damien turns up the volume on the side of his phone and the speakers start to play. There's talking, it's Bella and Chloe. "Oh Damien, what did you do." I chuckle. The app turns Bella's phone microphone on and Damien can listen to her surroundings without her being notified. We can hear them talking and they sound ok, but we can't quite make out what they are saying. Damien connects his phone to the car, we then hear Chloe's voice crystal clear. "Every time I see him, I want to rip his clothes off, cover him in Nutella and lick it off!!" Jealousy runs through me. Who is she talking about!? She sounds drunk. "Maybe we should just go inside and get them."

"No!" I say firmly, grabbing his arm to stop him from reaching the phone. I need to know who the hell she is talking about. "It's the best, that and cookie dough ice cream. Yeah, I want to cover Josh in Nutella, lick it off and then ride him while eating cookie dough ice cream. Nutella, ice cream and Josh. Heaven!" Did she just say Josh? I look at Damien and he has an amused smirk on his face. She definitely said Josh. Bella then speaks and Damien's amused expression turns to anger. I missed what she said fully as I was running Chloe's words through my head. All I caught was, something about not telling Damien as he will be angry. Too late for that, he's out of the car and storming into the restaurant.

Chapter 3

Josh

"Stop treating me like a child. You're not my dad. Never had one, never needed one." We've never had a conversation about our parents. I gathered Chloe's parents weren't in the picture as she hasn't ever spoken of them, only ever of her grandma. She makes me so mad. Stop treating her like a child she says. Chloe has never looked more like one than at this moment. Slumped in the car seat, sulking with her arms crossed. I'd love nothing more than to spank her bottom right now. Teach her a lesson for making me crazy. "I'm only looking out for you Clo. You've just been through a traumatic experience. Alcohol is not a good idea."

"Well, I happen to think it's just what I need, Thank you! Plus, we were celebrating." She's so stubborn, and so drunk. As I drive back to Damien's Chloe falls asleep. I wonder what they were celebrating? and what she couldn't tell Damien? I'm sure I will find out soon enough.

We arrive at the house and Chloe is still asleep. I try and wake her but she's not for moving. I consider what to do for the best. I can't really leave her here all night. I'd have to stay with her, and I don't fancy that. Then again if I carry her in, she might go mental at me again for holding her. I decide to take the risk. I take a deep breath and carry her in. She will just have to deal with it.

Chloe doesn't wake up until we reach her bedroom. I place her on the bed waiting the backlash. Chloe's eyes dart open and she gets up off the bed. "Josh, oh Josh come here." She drapes her arms around me stumbling a little. "I think you should get into bed Clo and try and get some sleep." "Goooood….. Idea! Lets go to bed." She looks at me trying to give me a wink, but ends up just blinking at me slowly with her mouth open. She cracks me up. Chloe begins to undress. I look away. Well, I might take a sneaky peak, I am a man after all. She is now completely naked. "Come on Josh, get undressed, lets go to bed." Chloe is lay in bed holding up the covers for me to get in.

"I don't think that's a good idea Clo. You get some rest and I will come and check on you in a bit." "Please Josh just come lie with me till I fall asleep?" Why can I not say no to this woman? Against my better judgment I take the covers and put them over her, then I lay on top of them next to her. I can not risk being so close to her with nothing in between us. I would never take advantage of Chloe when she has had a drink. Plus when we do have our first time together, I want Chloe to remember every second. And there will be a first time, and many more times after that. I am sure of it now, after hearing her speak about me with Bella today. Chloe snuggles up to me and falls asleep. She smells amazing. I put my face in her hair and inhale. I close my eyes and think of Nutella and cookie dough ice cream growing as hard as a rock.

I wake up and the room is pitch black. Its midnight. Which means I have been asleep for 6 hours. I can't remember the last time slept that long, especially not all in one go. Chloe is still asleep. I watch her for a few minutes. I can just make out her face with the moonlight coming in from the window. It's taking all my strength not to kiss her. I decide to go to the gym and workout. I need to clear my head. Damien's already in there letting off some steam. He's got music blaring and he's going full throttle on the treadmill. He slows it down when he sees me enter. "Hey mate how's it going?" I know there's something on his mind.

"Great. It's been a hell of a night."

"Oh yeah?"

"Since I last saw you, I've gone from Damien the boyfriend to Damien the husband and daddy to be." He rakes his hand through his hair, looking a bit panicked. I laugh. "Well congratulations, you don't do anything by halves do you!" I slap him on the back and pull him in for a hug. He's so tense.

"Tell me what's on your mind?" Damien pulls out of my hug and looks me seriously in the eyes.

"How do I do it Josh? How do I protect Bella……..and a baby?" I laugh again. He's got it so bad. At first I thought he was mental, worrying so much over Bella. Her safety has become his

25

obsession. But I'm starting to get it. I'm feeling it with Chloe. It's like this primal instinct takes over your body and there's nothing you can do to stop it. Every part of you from your brain to your c**k wants to worship and protect every part of her. "You've a whole team of trained protectors. They'll be perfectly fine. How do you think other dads do it."

We lift some weights and I think I manage to calm Damien down from his wobble. Damien calls it a night and I go to my room to shower. On my way I hear Chloe shouting for help. I run as fast as I can to her room. I find her in bed thrashing about crying. She's having a nightmare again. "Hey Clo, it's ok, it's ok Chloe. You're ok" I sit on the bed next to her, I have learnt my lesson. I won't be picking her up. I reach out and touch her face. One of her hands grabs mine, then she sits bolt up right and punches me in the nose with the other. Ouch!! That f**king hurt. Chloe then opens her eyes realising what she has done. She climbs out of bed standing in front of me. "Oh Josh I'm so sorry, are you ok? Let me see." She puts the bedside light on and.........oh wow. My breath is taken away. Her hands cup my face as she looks at my nose. But I can't take my eyes off her perfect, naked body. She checks me over for a minute and then looks at herself, realising her lack of clothing. "Hold on a minute. Why am I naked? What were you doing to me?" This dam woman. How dare she accuse me of such a thing. I can't speak to her. I get up and leave the room before I bend her over that bed and f**k her into next week. Does she not realise how much she means to me. "Don't you walk away from me Josh. Come back here, I want to talk to you!" I slam my bathroom door and get into the shower.

Chloe

How dare he walk away from me. I put on my jeans and a vest top and I follow him into his bedroom. It's empty. I walk into his bathroom without thinking and find him wet and soapy in the shower. The shower screen is steamed up but I can still make out the outline of his large muscular body. My eyes roam over him taking all of him in. Josh wipes the steam off the screen with one hand. Now I can see what stands at his groin. He is rock hard. "Come here Clo." He instructs. I move closer to the shower. He steps out slightly, grabs my arm and pulls me under the water fully clothed. Pushing me against the wall he takes my hands in his and holds them above my head. He pushes himself into my crotch. I couldn't move if I wanted to, which I don't. "Do you see what you do to me?!" His voice is almost a growl, I feel the vibrations all through my body. "You drive me crazy." His nose and lips brush against mine. "Do you want this Clo?" He pushes himself into me further. Oh my god do I want this? I can't take my eyes from his, they're deep and full of desire. I lean forward and take his lips in mine. He's as hungry for me as I am for him. We kiss and explore each other's mouths and it's just as delicious as I imagined, if not more so. I'm still pinned to the wall with my hands above my head, the loss of control adds to my desire. He breaks our kiss, nose to nose he says "If we do this Clo, I will be marking you as mine. Complete fidelity on both parts. Do you understand me? Once we do this you belong to me. I do not share." His words are everything that I would usually fight against. I have never belonged to anyone, never obeyed anyone, especially not a man. But right now, I would give my soul to the devil to have him inside me. "Take me, Josh!" As soon as I say those words it is like I have unveiled a beast. His alpha has been released and I am his prey ready for the taking. My top is pulled over my head, my jeans unfastened. Letting go of my hands, he crouches before me. Slowly removing my jeans he helps me out of them. His hands trail up my body as he stands. Tingles run through me following his touch. Our lips meet again and we devour each other. I want more, I need more. I push my body into him. His hands squeeze my bum, he lifts me, and my legs automatically wrap around him. My back is against the tiled wall. It's cold, which adds to the many sensations my body is already feeling. Josh rubs his hard length between me. I'm so hot and ready for him. I don't think I can hold out for much longer. Josh holds my jaw stopping me from moving my head "look at me!" I don't take my eyes from his. He watches me intensely as he slides in. A wave of something incredible rips through my body, it's pleasure, emotion, fulfilment. I watch Josh's eyes as they turn a darker shade of blue. He makes me feel like I'm the sexiest woman on the planet. With every thrust he goes deeper, stretching and filling me with the most delightful burn. We touch and explore each other's bodies while still remaining eye contact. I'm almost at my climax as Josh begins to quicken his pace. I know he is almost there, so I let myself lose control. It starts in my toes, shaking and tingling working it's way up my legs. The heat and pulse then explode between my legs, squeezing the hard length inside me. Josh now loses control, his body tenses, he's pounding so hard. It's slower and forceful, it's incredible. His eyes grow even darker until they roll back in his head. He then let's out the sexiest noise I have ever heard. "Clo. What have you done to me." He rests his head on my shoulder. I put my arms around him and kiss his neck, still shaking from the most intense orgasm. After a minute he puts me down, still holding me as I'm a little off balance. Josh turns off the shower, steps out and gets a towel which he holds out for me. He is still standing completely naked and wet through. Mmmm I could definitely have another go on that. I step out and let him wrap me up. We dry ourselves off, both catching each other's eyes and giving each other a little smirk as we do. I can't believe what just happened. Don't get me wrong, I wanted this to happen. I've dreamed of this happening, but I just can't believe it happened now, tonight. Josh climbs into his bed and holds the covers back for me. I shrug, why not. I climb in the crisp white sheets and snuggle up to him. We share a few kisses and then fall asleep in each other's arms.

Josh

I've done it again. I've fallen asleep without even trying and slept for 6 hours. I must be careful. I too have nightmares where I can thrash out. I'd hate to hurt Chloe while I was asleep. I am shocked at how easily I have fallen asleep.

Chloe stirs at the side of me. She is incredible. God, I think back to last night in the shower. That wasn't how I wanted our first time to be. But she blew my mind. She's a stubborn, sexy, argumentative little minx and I can't get enough of her. I hope I wasn't too rough with her. I couldn't help myself, she drives my body crazy. Those piercing green eyes see into my soul. Her dark shiny hair, olive skin and freckles. She's a perfect beauty. My manhood is awake and wanting more, her scent is turning me on. I need a distraction. She's too peaceful to disturb and I want to be here when she wakes up. I decide to stay in bed and work from my phone. Another hour or so passes and Chloe wakes up. She's got a smile on her face that matches mine. "Good morning baby how did you sleep?" I turn on my side to face her. I run my fingers down her side, watching the goosebumps arise following my touch. "I slept ok, apart from when you were snoring." She rolls her eyes and turns putting her back to me with a smirk on her face. I do not snore. Well I don't think I do. I pull the covers off her to reveal her perfect body. That ass. "Hey! I'm cold!" She giggles trying to pull the covers back. I wrap my body around her, pressing my length into her bum crack. "I'll warm you up baby!" Chloe sighs and pushes her body back into mine. I think we are a go for morning love making. I begin by kissing the side of her neck. The little appreciative noises she makes are sexy as hell. I massage her shoulders, back and bum. I can sense her arousal is peaking, so I turn her head and roll her on her back. I place my body over the front of hers. She feels amazing, our skin to skin. My needy girl keeps pushing her body into me. I need to savour this though, for a little longer yet. I sit up with my legs either side of hers. Chloe grabs my length and begins to pump. "No Clo. Not yet." I remove her hands and place them both above her head. "Keep them here." My hands caress her body. Rubbing and squeezing. My mouth kisses and tastes, until I can't do anything more than get inside her. I'm gentle and slower this time. I stroke myself through her a few times and then sink in. I watch her facial expressions as I do. I'm at the peak of arousal and I need to devour her. Chloe's hands roam my body. Her touch is electric. The groans and noises coming from my mouth are sounds I've never heard from myself before. She does this to me. She makes me lose control. "Josh!" My name on her lips sends me into ecstasy. "Come with me baby!" We both convulse, scream and consume each other. It's hot as hell.

We hold each other until our bodies calm down. I roll off her and slide out realising something. "I'm so sorry Clo. I haven't used protection." Chloe smiles at me and strokes my face, I kiss the palm of her hand, her touch is magical. "It's ok, I'm on the pill and I'm clean."

"Good, but I shouldn't have assumed. You make me so crazy Clo, I lose all common sense when I'm around you. And I'm clean too, it's been a long time." Why did I tell her that. What is happening to me. Whenever I'm around her I lose control of my senses. I need to get a grip. I'm turning into Damien. F**k. "What are your plans for today?"

"I think I'm just going stay here. Use the gym, go for a swim have a relax in the garden. I'll see what Bella is doing."

"Ok, I've got to go in the office today. Promise me if you change your plans, you will tell me?" Clo looks at me with her disobedient look.

"Josh you do not need to babysit me. I am perfectly fine."

"Don't fight me on this Clo, I just want to know where you are."

"Fine, if I go out I'll let you know. But I'm not going anywhere so no need to worry. And on that note, I'm off." She jumps out of bed. Puts on her jeans and top and leaves the room, blowing me a kiss as she closes the door. I chuckle. What a woman.

I'm glad Chloe is staying here. I've got some things to do today that can't wait so I can't watch out for her. I would have got one of the guys to tail her if needed but I don't trust anyone as much as I trust myself to protect her. The Manor House is like Fort Knox so I'm happy with that.

Damien's taken Bella for a scan this morning so I'm on my own dealing with a nightmare situation. We have 3 teams of men. There are 2 shifts of 12 hours. The purpose of having 3 teams is so there will always be a few guys in case of emergency, back up and sickness. Last night 2 of my teams decided to go out for a curry for one of the lad's birthdays. 80% of them have now got food poisoning and are fit for nothing. I'm livid. They've put people's lives and my business at major risk with this brainless decision. I can't trouble Damien this morning, but I hope he hurries up.

I spend the morning rearranging and reducing teams, we have most jobs covered to some extent. When I eventually get a minute to think, my mind goes straight to Chloe. Her storming into my bathroom. I'd gone in there to cool off. Her argumentative and stubbornness drive me mad, but turn me on like someone possessed. I have never felt like this about anyone. It's insane. I check my phone and see a message from her.

CHLOE: Thanks for last night and this morning. It was just what I needed xx

What?! Thanks!? I hope she doesn't think this was

a one off. There's no going back from this now. It's sounds crazy, but I meant it when I said she is mine now.

Chloe

Wow. I feel incredible. Josh was everything I imagined and more. I felt things I never had with anyone else. Not that I've been in a serious relationship before. I've dated a lot and been with guys for a while, but no one I could see any future with. I'm not sure I see a future with Josh. He infuriates me when he tries to control me and expects me to do everything he asks. But I can't get enough of him. I already miss him. My body craves his touch. I've text him but he hasn't replied. He said last night in the shower that I had to agree to be his, to fidelity. I agreed as I was so hungry for him. I'm not sure whether it was just some strange dirty talk he likes or whether he actually meant it. Each to their own, it worked for me.

I'm in the gym running my ass off. I hadn't thought of the shooting incident since yesterday. Josh had completely taken over my mind. The sickness and guilt feeling return. I can't stop thinking about what I could have done to stop Tyler being killed.

My phone pings with a message. I stop the treadmill and get off. I'm wet through. My legs are jelly. I've been on it for over an hour and I think I've overdone it. It's a message on Facebook. It's Tyler's grandma. She wants to meet me. I'm not sure it's a good idea or what I will say to her, but it's the least I can do I suppose. I have a shower and get dressed. I pull up to the manor gates in my yellow mini, well it was Bella's but she gave it to me. I wouldn't have chosen yellow but it reminds me of her, so I love it. There's only one security guard on today and he lets me out no questions asked. I suddenly remember the promise I made to Josh about letting him know if I went out. I will let him know when I get there as my phone is in my bag in the back. To be honest I bet the manor security are on the phone to him now grassing me up anyway. Honestly, I can't cope with this. The sooner I find my own place the better.

Chapter 4

Chloe

Tyler's grandma wants to meet me in the coffee shop down the road from the youth centre. I need to drive past the centre to get to the coffee shop. As I approach, I can feel my heart beating in my chest. I don't get anxious so this is an unusual experience. I suppose this is how Bella feels. She has always suffered from anxiety. The centre is cordoned off with police tape. There are 2 policemen standing outside. I continue down the road trying to keep it together. I find a parking space outside the coffee shop and go in. I'm not sure what Tyler's grandma looks like, and I'm a bit early, so I assume she's not here yet. I get a latte, find a table in the back and message her to say I'm here. I have no idea what I am going to say to this woman. What if she gets angry with me for not saving him. He was my responsibility after all. I wouldn't blame her.

A woman looking lost with puffy eyes walks in. I give her a wave and she walks over "Chloe?"

"Yeah I'm Chloe. Let me get you a drink." I stand and she asks for a tea. I order and bring it back to our table. "Thank you for meeting me. I know this must be difficult for you. The police told me how wonderful you were with all the children and that Tyler unfortunately couldn't be helped." Both of our eyes fill with tears, I give her hand a squeeze while she composes herself.

"I just need to understand what happened and why. The police have been very vague in what they have told me."

Joan is the lady's name and she reminds me so much of my grandma. She too brought Tyler up by herself. Tyler's mum had been a teenager when he was born and had left him with her. My mother had passed away shortly after I was born. Tyler hadn't known his father either like myself, so he'd unfortunately looked for that male influence in the wrong people. We talk for a couple of hours. Joan tells me stories of Tyler growing up and I share my experiences of him clowning around and cheering everyone up. I've told Joan all that happened. I'm not sure whether it has helped or not but I'm glad I came. I decide to get another coffee when she leaves. I sit and people watch for a while.

I'm about to get up and leave when I feel a presence behind me. Someone puts their mouth to my ear and I feel something hard poke me between my shoulder blades.

"What you can feel in your back is a full size pistol. You know the one, you filmed me using a couple of days ago and gave to the police." The whisper in my ear makes my skin crawl. "I am sure you will believe me when I say I will not hesitate to use it, on you or anyone else that stands in my way. So, for the sake of all the other people and kids in this coffee shop, I suggested you do as I ask. Do you understand?" I nod, and take a deep breath trying not to panic.

For goodness sake. If this guy doesn't kill me, Josh will for getting myself into this mess. I'm doubting he knows that I left since I haven't had any calls from him. Well, that might not be a bad thing.

"Now. Leave your phone on the table and walk out of the front door. But do it slowly, so I can stay close behind you." I stand slowly and look around at the other people enjoying their refreshments. None of them have noticed the situation I am in. I thought maybe I could alert them with my eyes or something, but nobody makes eye contact with me. We exit onto the street.

"Turn right."

I walk down the pavement, again trying to catch the eye of someone for help, but nobody looks at me, or if they do, they don't have a clue what's going on. We reach a white transit van.

"Stop here."

He opens the back doors and instructs me in. I get in the empty, fish smelling van and sit on the wet floor. The doors are shut, and I'm left in darkness.

The van's engine starts, I feel it pull out into the London traffic. We are moving slowly, stopping and starting. I wonder whether to bang on the door and shout for help. Surely cars at the side of us will hear me. It's just if he gets mad before anyone can help and goes on a shooting spree. Then again what is his plan with me anyway? He's obviously furious I filmed him, and I'm the only witness. He's not going to give me a slap on the wrist and let me go, is he? I'm mulling my options over when I hear the van door open, then close. The van is still moving slowly so I know it's not him getting out. I can hear voices. I move to the back of the van and put my ear to the wall between us. The guy is talking to someone else in the van, this person is talking more quietly, they obviously know I am here. I listen.

"I don't care who the f**k she is!"..........

"Not a f**king chance!"..............

"Get lost Dad, I told you it's never going to happen! .... Get out!"

I hear the other voice quietly continue in protest.

"Shit! It's f**king Tom Hardy here to ruin my day!"

The front doors to the van open again.

There's shouting.

*BANG *BANG *BANG!!! That ear piercing sound of a gun I have heard far too many times.

I cover my ears and close my eyes. I think of good thoughts to take my mind off the situation.

It's silent for a few minutes until a loud crack makes me jump. The back doors of the van open. It's been so dark in here the light blinds my eyes.

It takes me a minute to focus and see, but I'd recognise that silhouette anywhere.

Josh.

I stand and look at him.

I realise the gunman was talking about Josh when he said Tom Hardy was here. He does have a look of him. He looks incredibly handsome standing there with the light beaming behind him, outlining his muscular frame.

His face however changes from relief to absolute fury.

Oh dear.

"Don't just stand there, get out!"

I quickly walk to the open doors. Josh leans in and grabs me around the tops of my legs and throws me over his shoulder. He carries me like this to his car, puts me in the passenger seat and gets in to drive. As he sits down, he winces. I notice the jeans on his left leg are covered in blood.

"Josh your bleeding. Are you ok, do you want me to drive?"

"No! I'm fine! It's just a flesh wound." He's so angry. Josh pulls out into the traffic, I notice that 2 cars pull out behind us.

"It's ok they're with us."

I keep quiet as I'm not sure what to say, I don't want to make Josh more angry. I contemplate thanking him for getting me out of there, but I think he may have a go at me for leaving the house. I just can't deal with that right now, so I stare out of the window and I don't say a word.

We arrive at Kingston manor, Damien and Bella are at the door to meet us.

"Glad to see you're ok Chloe. Come on mate let's get

you sorted out, the medical team is here." Damien and Josh disappear into the lift. I mean seriously, who has a lift in their house, I still can't get used to it.

"My god Chloe, you need to stop scaring me like this." She pulls me in for a hug.

"I'm sorry Bella. I shouldn't be worrying you like this. How are you? how's the baby? Do you have photos?" I pull Bella into the sitting room. I suddenly feel exhausted.

We sit on the sofa, and I'm explained to in detail how the scan was performed. How it felt, what it sounded like, how it looked, what Bella felt like etc etc. When Bella tells a story, she tells you every detail, which I love, especially at this moment in time, it takes my mind off my crazy few days.

Josh comes in a couple of hours later and brings me back to reality.

"The police are on their way. They need to take your statement." Oh no, not again. I hate having to relive everything.

The police are here and have been questioning me for over an hour. Josh is sat beside me.

"So it was a male you heard enter the vehicle?"

"Yes, I think so."

"And how old do you think this male was?"

"I'm not sure. It was a man's voice, so not a teenager, but other than that I have no idea."

"And what did you hear them say?"

"I couldn't make out what the other man said, I

could hear him talking but not what he said."

"Ok, tell me what you heard your abductor say?"

"Something along the lines of :

I don't care who the f**k she is.

Not a f**king chance!

Oh and then:

Get lost Dad, I told you it's never going to happen.

"He called him dad?" Josh stiffens and shoots a look at Damien who is stood in the doorway listening. Damien then disappears. "Yes, I think so. I could be mistaken though."

"And is that all?"

"Yes, apart from him shouting that Tom Hardy was here to ruin his day, which I assume was Josh."

After talking to the police, I realise how lucky I have been again, and that the reason I am still alive is because of Josh.

The police leave and Josh and I are left alone in the sitting room.

"How are you? How's your leg?" Josh doesn't look at me. He just rubs his forehead and speaks.

"It's fine."

"Josh, please look at me." He slowly looks at me and my heart breaks a little. His look is just pure disappointment. He hasn't even let me explain though. I didn't plan to go out, it was only because Tyler's grandma asked me to meet her. I thought the manor security would have told him I was leaving. Before I can explain, Josh stands "You need to pack a bag. We are going away for a while."

"What? Where?"

"It doesn't matter where. Just pack a bag and do it quickly." He exits the room leaving me furious.

I go to my room and start throwing clothes and toiletries in a suitcase. I'm livid. Livid Josh thinks he can just tell me what to do. Livid I am actually doing what he says, and livid my life has turned out this way and I don't really have any option. A little knock at my door brings me out of my strop.

"Hey Bella, come in."

"Damien says you're going away for a bit until things calm down here?"

"So I've been told, yes."

"You know they wouldn't do this unless absolutely necessary, and all Josh wants is for you to be safe." I slump onto my bed.

"I know, it's just so hard Bella. I've never had anyone so involved in my life before, telling me what to do and when to do it." Bella sits beside me and pulls me in for a cuddle.

"You've spent all your life looking after other people, me and your grandma. Now it's time to let someone look after you." I squeeze Bella back. I know she's right, but I don't know if I can change a habit of a lifetime. "I'm going to miss you Bella."

"I'll miss you more. Has Josh told you where you're going? Damien said it's better if I don't know."

"He hasn't said."

"Right well you should think of it as an adventure holiday. No work for a while, go and explore a new place and spend some time with a sexy man who adores you." This makes me laugh.

"I'm not sure he adores me right now."

"He will calm down. Now let me help you pack."

Bella cheers me up, I feel a bit more positive, or rather a bit less negative now about my trip. I've just about got everything packed and Josh appears at my door. "You ready to go Clo?"

"All set. I'll call you when we get there, wherever there is. Oh no I haven't got my phone it's in the coffee shop" I look at Josh.

"We will sort you a new one when we can." I give Bella the biggest hug.

"You look after yourself and my nephew or niece in there."

Josh loads the car and we set off in silence. Part of me is mad with him and the other part is crazy hot for him. He's sat in the driving seat of his Range Rover. His tight dark blue jeans cling to his muscular thighs. He's got a bright white t-shirt on that accentuates his tanned strong arms. And he's wearing Ray-bans. Hot…...as…….. hell!

We drive for about 10 mins and pull into an underground car park. 4 floors down we stop at a locked, roller, garage door. Josh gets out and opens it. Inside there is another car under a sheet. He begins to unload our boot. Having not said a word I assume we are changing car, so I get out and help unload. Once the car is unloaded Josh removes the sheet from the car. It's an old black Porsche. It's beautiful and shiny, obviously has been well looked after. "Wow."

"Yeah. She was my dad's." He gets in and pulls it

out of the garage, he then parks the range in and locks it up. Once we've loaded the Porsche, we set off again. "This is a beautiful car Josh. Do you drive it often?"

"No, I don't. I have never driven it other than to park it in the garage after my dad died."

"So why today?"

"The car isn't registered to me, so it will be easier to get out of the area unnoticed. I've been waiting for an excuse to drive it."

"Thank you, Josh. And for what it's worth, I'm sorry." He looks at me over his sunglasses, grunts and then looks back at the road. He's so stubborn, well that's the last time I am apologising.

We drive for a couple of hours in silence. I try and distract myself from the hunk sitting at the side of me but it's extremely difficult. He smells incredible and it does all sorts of things to my senses. He is so dam hot. Women walking past or in cars next to us can't stop staring at him and I'm feeling rather jealous. I just want to grab him and snog his face off to show them that he is mine. But is he mine? Last night in the shower he said that I was his, but is he mine? It's like he hates me, like I'm the biggest inconvenience to him. It's getting me all wound up thinking about it. We had the most amazing night and morning together and now this. That bloody gunman, not only has he murdered those boys and tried to kidnap me, but he's also c**k blocking me and I'm furious!

The car pulls into a petrol station. Josh says we

will be travelling through the night and he will get us some food. Next to the petrol station, I notice there's an off-license. Just what I need.

Chapter 5

Chloe

I wander in and have a look around. A bottle of wine might help take my mind off Mr Grumpy and send me off to sleep. I choose a Pinot Grigio with a screw top. "Do you have any straws?" I ask the guy at the till. "Classy lady, just what I like." He laughs. "Yep that's me."

"No sorry I don't think we have." Oh well, it won't be the first time I've drank from the bottle.

"Have you any I.D miss?" It's a while since I have been asked for identification. Feeling rather flattered I hand him my driving license.

"Chloe, a pretty name for a pretty lady." This guy is definitely flirting with me, but he's too young and scrawny for me.

"WHAT THE HELL IS GOING ON!" Josh reaches over me and snatches my driving license out of the guy's hand. "GET IN THE CAR!" Oh god, here he is again Mr grumpy. I decide not to argue and do as he says.

"Hey miss, are you ok?" He's obviously concerned with Josh's angry out bust.

"I'm fine thanks, my 'dad' here just doesn't like me drinking." Josh snorts and scowls at me as he escorts me out. He's a pain in my ass but I love when he gets all alpha male.

We get in the car, and I open my wine taking a big gulp.

"Seriously Clo?! We are trying to go somewhere without being traced and you're just handing your driving license out to whoever the F**k asks for it!"

S**t I didn't think about that.

"He won't remember me in an hour so anyway"

"Are you for real? You're gorgeous Clo! The image of you in those skinny jeans, is going to be burned in his memory forever. And I f**king hate it." He bangs his fists on the steering wheel.

Josh

This woman is going to be the death of me. All I want to do is protect her, she makes me so crazy I want to put her over my knee and punish her. She's like a wild animal that can't be tamed.

I'm driving us to a quiet seaside, fishing village. It's on the south east coast, my dad used to take me there when I was a boy. That's if I've not killed Chloe myself before we get there. She's a fiery little minx I don't why I'm so attracted to her.

I put some music on to distract myself and calm down. It works for a while until Chloe has consumed half of the bottle of wine. She obviously is feeling the effects of the alcohol now as she starts to move her body to the music and sing a little. I try not to look, but she is so sexy.

"So where are we going?" Chloe asks and I'm

grateful for the distraction.

"It's a small seaside town. It's quiet, not an obvious place to go and there are a few easy routes, out of there, one being by sea. I used to go there with my dad years ago."

"Are you close to your dad?"

"Yeah, very close, and my mum too. Unfortunately, my dad passed away when I was a teenager. I've many great memories of him, he made me who I am. I don't get to see mum as much as I'd like, I should really make more of an effort to see her I suppose."

"That's a shame about your dad. It's nice you were close though, I never knew my parents, my grandma brought me up."

"I'm sorry I didn't know Clo."

"No need to be sorry, I've never known any different, and my grandma did a great job. She passed away about 6 months ago, but she had a good life. I miss her, but it is what it is."

"So, what happened to your parents then?"

"My mum died when I was a baby, she had a blood condition, and I never knew my father. My grandma never knew either. I think it was a one-night stand for my mother, and she didn't for whatever reason know who my father was."

"Have you ever tried to find out who your dad was?"

"No, I literally know nothing about him."

"If you want to, I will do all I can to help you get some answers. We have a good private investigation team and I have ways and means of finding information out." Chloe gives me a smile.

"Thanks Josh. I'm not sure I want to know but thank you for the offer. I'll definitely think about it."

I manage to persuade Chloe to not drink any more wine. She also listens when I explain how serious the situation is, and that she really must do what I say. I hadn't wanted to worry her at first, but she's been so blasé about the whole situation I have had to hit her with some reality.

I drive for a few more hours while Chloe sleeps. As I pull off the motorway, I recognise the winding country roads. It brings back memories of my father. We used to come here twice a year, just me and him. We'd go fishing and surfing together. Dad had a busy job and worked away a lot, but he always made sure we spent quality time together and I had his undivided attention.

The roads turn narrower as we get nearer to our destination. I smell the sea before I see it. I'm overcome with emotion. The roads open up onto the seafront. The sun is beginning to rise. This is my happy place. I hear a noise at the side of me and see Chloe is starting to wake up. I'm grateful for being in a beautiful place with an even more beautiful girl. I just hope I can keep her safe.

"Wow. It's so pretty Josh." Chloe sits up so she can take in the view. "Look at those beach huts all different colours it looks like something off a postcard." Chloe's right it does look spectacular, with the sun coming up shining a warm light that sparkles on the sea, it would be an ideal picture. We drive down the seafront, Chloe has her window down with her face in the wind smiling as she takes it all in. "Please tell me we are staying in one of those huts Josh."

"Nope." Chloe slumps back in her seat.

"So where are we staying then?"

"Here." I say as I pull around the bend and drive down the beach to a row of 5 pastel coloured beach cottages.

"Wow!"

I get the key out of the key safe by the door and l have a quick check inside before I let Chloe in.

She looks around the cottage in absolute awe. I watch as the magic of the cottage takes her breath away. I smile as I remember how I felt exactly like that as a kid every time I came here. It's not a big place, although, for the price of it, it should be. But you can't beat the location. There's a cosy living area with an open kitchen diner. The bathroom is on the ground floor with just a shower, toilet and sink. Upstairs there are 2 double bedrooms. At the front, a large decking area with a table, chairs and a hammock look out to sea. Me and dad spent many evenings sitting out there playing cards and talking about our day's events.

Chloe puts the kettle on while I unload the car. "I've put you in the room on the right and me on the left. They're both identical really." Chloe gives me funny look. I don't know whether it's because I put us in separate rooms or if she wanted to choose herself, but I didn't want to assume. Plus, I don't want to make a habit of spending the night with Chloe, I can't risk having a nightmare and hurting her. I at least need to speak to her about it first, so she knows what to expect.

We drink our tea sat out on the decking, watching the sunrise. Chloe looks relaxed and happy. I've always wanted to come back here with someone that meant something to me. I just wish it was under happier circumstances.

"I'm going to freshen up then can we go for a walk? I can't wait to see more of the place." I nod. I can't wait to show her more.

I shower and change too, I'm feeling surprisingly awake considering I haven't slept but that's usual for me. I'm out on the front waiting, when Chloe joins me. She's wearing a little sundress and her hair is down and flowing. She takes my breath away. I feel my pants growing tighter by the sight of her. I'm not sure I want her walking around looking like that, I don't want anyone looking at what's mine.

Chloe

We walk along the beach paddling in the sea. I enjoy feeling the cold water and sand between my toes. It's a long time since I went to the seaside.

It's a beautiful morning. It's July and the weather has been really good recently. I think the weather is always better on the coast. Josh tells me about how he used to surf here with his dad. I'm enjoying listening to him. He's letting his guard down and showing me his softer side that I know is underneath. That is until we reach the village, and he turns all bodyguard mode. Honestly, it's laughable. He's now got his sunglasses on with his stern 'don't mess with me' expression. His arm is around me holding my upper arm and he's guiding me around people like I'm some kind of celebrity working our way through rowdy fans. "Hey, Josh?" I stop and he raises his sunglasses to look at me. "We are safe here? Right?" He looks at me and nods. "Right well, you're drawing attention to us acting like this, so let's just slow it down. Let me link you." I move his arm from around me and link it with mine. "See that's better. Much more natural, and, I'm still just as close to you." I smile, but he just huffs and lowers his sunglasses back over his eyes. He's a grump, but I'll take that as a small win.

We stroll around, in and out of the little shops. One of them is an antique jewellery shop. It's full of beautiful unique pieces. I spot a brooch identical to one my grandma used to wear. "Oh wow, Josh. My grandma used to have one just like this. My grandpa bought it for her. But it was stolen while we were on holiday once." I smile to myself, but feel a little sad. I do miss her. I pick up the brooch and turn it around in my fingers. It's platinum, a star or a flower I could never make my mind up which. It's covered with diamonds and a Pearl in the middle. I put it back when I notice the price. No wonder it was stolen, they won the lottery when they took that.

I keep wandering around the shop enjoying the beauty of each piece, thinking about the people who wore them previously.

A bracelet with 3 blue diamonds catches my eye. I've never seen blue diamonds before. They're deep and mesmerising, they remind me of Josh's eyes.

"Hey, what you looking at?"

"This bracelet. Blue diamonds, it's the first time I've ever seen them. They remind me of your eyes." Josh looks at me, giving me a little smirk just as one of the shop assistants joins us. "I see your admiring the blue diamonds. These are extremely rare. Especially blue of this intensity. The bracelet chain is broken unfortunately but the diamonds could be removed and made into any sort of jewellery. I can do you a good price." I almost have a heart attack upon hearing the amount.

"I'll get it for you if you like?"

"Don't be ridiculous Josh. I know you're not short of a bob or two but that's insane." I pull Josh out of the shop, and we continue with our walk.

There's a bakery up ahead, the smell of freshly baked bread draws us to it. I get a couple of pastries and Josh gets an extra large barm cake filled with bacon and sausage. He devours it in minutes while window shopping. The village is so beautiful. It's all cream stone buildings and pale pastel coloured doors. Josh is starting to relax a little. I'm really enjoying our morning together. I know we aren't here on holiday, but I do believe everything happens for a reason. I'm meant to be here now with Josh. I know there's some psycho after me that wants to kill me, but all the more reason to enjoy life now. 'When your times up, your times up'.

Josh takes me to the harbour. He talks about his father and their time together. We stop at the fishing marina. There are family generations sitting together, the older ones giving the younger one's advice on how to cast and reel it in. I catch Josh smiling at the sight obviously reliving memories. On the walk back to the cottage we pass a phone shop. "Can I just go in here Josh and get a new phone?"

"No!" I stop and look at him to get an explanation for his outburst. "You don't need a phone. Phone calls can be traced. I'll be with you at all times so no need to have one."

"But what about Bella? I need to phone Bella, she will be worrying about me, wondering where we are."

"It's best if she doesn't know where we are. Damien will keep her updated and let her know that you are safe."

"And how will Damien know? Do you have a phone? Because I don't think that's very fair!" I put my hands on my hips. "I have ways of contacting Damien which are untraceable. Don't give me that attitude little lady."

"Oh yeah, what are you going do about it?"

His eyebrows raise above his sunglasses. Maybe I shouldn't have pushed him. Josh bends and throws me over his shoulder. "Put me down." I half shout, half-laugh. He heads out of the village towards the beach and our cottage. I have a fine view of his arse in this position, so I am just enjoying the ride. I realise however that we have gone passed the row of cottages and are heading towards the sea. "Don't you dare Josh!" I kick and wriggle, but he just tightens his grip without saying a word. Josh walks into the sea still with his shoes on. I'm then thrown into the air and land in the freezing cold sea. My head goes under the water and I'm hit with brain freeze. I frantically get up, the temperature has taken my breath away. I stumble in the waves but finally get my balance. When I wipe my I eyes I see a very smug looking Josh staring at me. "You idiot!" I shout. "Aren't you supposed to be looking after me? Not trying to kill me!"

"You can swim, can't you?" He shouts as he walks out of the water. I don't think so mate. I run at him and jump on his back trying to put him down into the sea. But it's like jumping on a brick wall. He doesn't falter in the slightest, just pulls me off his back and throws me into the water, again. When I get up this time, I see him jogging down the beach. I set off running. He may be stronger than me, but I am definitely faster. My dress is heavy with it being wet through, so I take it off while running. I throw it at the back of his head and then run straight passed him in just my underwear.

"Hey! Get back here Clo!" Josh sounding his usual aggravated self.

After a while, I slow down to let Josh catch up with me. I'm interested in seeing what he will do to me next. With powerful strides, he approaches me. Putting his large hands on each side of my face he pulls me in for the most passionate and hungry kiss I've had in my life. Tingles spread throughout my body. My heart does a weird summersault type feeling that I haven't felt before. I can't be falling for a grumpy giant, surely not. Josh breaks our kiss. He then takes his top off revealing his large shoulders and chiselled chest. Yum. He pulls his T-shirt over my head feeding my arms through. We walk back to the cottage hand in hand not speaking a word. Anticipation of what's to come fulfils me. We both pick up our pace the close we get to the cottage. Josh obviously feeling the same as me. As soon as the door is closed Josh has me up against it. "I told you Clo. You are mine now." His face is pressed up against mine as he speaks. "Nobody gets to look at you like this, apart from me." He reaches down and pulls his T-shirt over my head. Moving back slightly his deep blue eyes roam my body. He ignites a fire inside me and I'm so hungry for him. I need my mouth on him. The feeling isn't something I've felt before. It's so strong and intense. I throw my arms around him, he picks me up as if I'm light as a feather. Kicking off his wet shoes, I'm carried upstairs to my room. Placing me by the side of my bed he stands looking at me, waiting for me to make the next move. I take off my wet bra and knickers. Josh's eyes are wide and his nostrils flare. I pull down Josh's shorts while he watches me. I go to take him in my hand but he grabs me and spins me around, my back against his warm hard chest. With his mouth next to my ear he says "I told you to be good Clo. Don't push me again. I don't like getting angry with you."

"Maybe I like you being angry with me" A quiet growl comes from Josh's throat. His mouth is on my neck, teeth and tongue gliding across my skin sending goosebumps down my body. Reaching around me he nestles his large hand in-between my legs. Massaging and stroking, making my legs quiver in the process. Kissing my neck and biting my ear. It doesn't take long for my body to start convulsing. When I'm almost there he stops and bends me over the bed. With my hands on the mattress holding myself up for support, he enters me with one deep thrust. I am filled with a euphoria I didn't realise I was missing. While massaging my insides with his hardness he squeezes my breasts and kisses my back. I catch the sight of us in the dressing table mirror. We look sooooo F**king Hot!! I can't believe it's me I'm watching with this incredible man. Josh turns to see what I'm looking at. He too is in awe of the sight of us. He gives me a dirty smile through the mirror, and he picks up his pace, the vision of us sparing him on. We look incredible. While holding eye contact we both reach our climax. Screaming out in pleasure we both slump to the bed. There's no going back from that magic we have just experienced together. I think Mr grump may be creeping into my heart.

Chapter 6

Chloe

We spend the rest of the day in bed making love. Loved is what I am feeling right now. It's quite surreal, a feeling I am not accustomed to. Once we are both completely worn out and hungry, we shower and get dressed for dinner. Josh takes me to a seafood restaurant on the harbour. We've held hands the whole way here, even now while seated opposite each other Josh won't let go of my hand. Something has changed between us today.

Josh orders for us both as I'm not sure what to get. I like fish but I've never been to a seafood restaurant. The waiter fills our table with of all sorts of fish and shellfish. Most of them I have never even heard of before. Josh teaches me how to season and eat oysters and how to get muscles out of their shell buy using another shell, it's quite a skill. Josh finds my lack of talent amusing. We are having a wonderful evening, laughing passing looks of longing to each other. I feel incredibly special.

"I almost forgot. I got something for you." Josh stands and reaches into his jeans pocket. He takes out a navy velvet box and hands it to me. I look at him in confusion. So many questions run through my head. When has he had chance to buy me a gift? Did he bring it with him? Isn't it a bit soon to be buying each other gifts? Maybe it's a small listening or tracking device he wants me to wear, that sounds more like it. With curious hands, I open it.

I'm shocked into silence by its contents. Tears stream from my eyes before I have chance to wipe them away. "Josh, you didn't have to do this."

"I did. I saw the happiness on your face when held the brooch in your hand. I want to always make you happy Clo." I take it out of the box and again I'm instantly brought images of my grandma full of smiles wearing the brooch with pride. "When did you even get it? You've not left my side?"

"While you were looking at the bracelet. I got one of the other shop assistants to serve me. I don't know how accurate she is, but she said that it is one of a kind, that it was a custom-made bespoke design. So, this could actually be your grandmas."

"Oh wow, I hope so Josh. Wouldn't that be amazing." I twist one side of my hair at the front and clip the brooch in my hair. I'm not a brooch wearing type of girl, but I love things in my hair. I look at my reflection in the window at the side of me, and for a second, I get a glimpse of my grandma.

After our meal, we walk along the beach and watch the sunset. This has been the best day of my life. "Thank you Josh. For bringing me here, for the brooch, for everything. I know I'm not the easiest of people. Thank you for sticking with me."

"You've got it all wrong. You're the one stuck with me Clo" Wrapping his arm around me and pulling me into him, he kisses me on top of my head.

When we arrive back at the cottage there's a guy on a ladder messing with something above the door. "Just in time mate. I'm all done here. If you check the app on your phone now it should be all up and running."

"New security system, cameras, and alarms." Josh explains to me. I nod and go inside to put the kettle on letting Josh finish speaking to the security guy.

We snuggle on the sofa for an hour watching the end of some action movie. I'm not at all interested in the film, I'm enjoying every second of breathing in this beautiful man.

We both start to yawn and agree it's bedtime. I'm looking forward to another love making session like we had earlier today. Surprisingly though, Josh leaves me at my bedroom door with a peck on the cheek, a good night, and his door locked behind him. What the hell?! I go into my room and slam the door. I stomp about getting undressed. We've had the most amazing day together and this is how he ends it?

Josh

I can hear Chloe stomping about in her room. I probably just dealt with that situation all wrong, but I know I'm in for a bad night tonight. It's been a while since I slept and I'm feeling exhausted, especially after today. That girl has ruined me. It was so hard leaving her tonight. All I want to do is have her in my arms but if I did that tonight, I'd hurt her. My nightmares have been an issue since my father was killed, but now they are even more of an inconvenience.

I should have explained this to Chloe, but I know she would have said it would be ok and persuaded me to sleep with her. And at this moment in time, I don't have the strength to resist. She will just have to have a strop tonight and I'll sort her out tomorrow, in more ways than one hopefully.

I give Damien a call. We've got radio phones which bounce the signal throughout the UK so they can't be traced. Damien informs me that he has found out who the gunman after Chloe is. It's only a matter of time now until we catch the bast**d.

As I expect I have a bad night. It takes me a few hours to actually get my body and mind to relax but when it does, I'm out for about 5 hours. I wake up on the floor with the contents of my bedside table around me. My whole body is sore, and I have a lump in the back of my head. I let myself come round for a few minutes on the floor, before I get up and tidy the mess I've made in the night. I quickly shower and go downstairs to find Chloe in the kitchen dancing to 'Un holy by Sam Smith'.

I stand in the doorway watching her jerk her hips to the music while sucking on a spoon covered in Nutella. I smile to myself remembering the little fantasy she told Bella about. That reminds me, I need a trip to the shops later. Proving to me once again how oblivious she is, I enjoy the view for a good couple of minutes.

When Chloe finally realises I'm standing here watching her, her face fills with a scowl and she stops dancing and starts stomping about making a brew.

"The kettles just boiled, you want one?" Well at least she's still talking to me, all be it grumpily.

"Yes please." I take a seat at the kitchen table. I decided to explain to Chloe about my sleeping habits. I briefly tell her what happened to my father, it haunts me that I still haven't been able to find out who killed him.

"I was 18. I woke in the night to the sound of men's voices. It was my dad and someone I didn't recognise. I went downstairs to investigate. As I reached the bottom step, I heard the gunshot I have never been able to get out of my mind. I ran to the kitchen where I found my dad lay on the tiled floor. In the corner of my eye, I saw a man leave through the back door. At the time my thoughts were only on my dad. In hindsight now I wish I had followed the man. My father was already dead. There was nothing I could do for him. The next day I decided I would never let anyone hurt my family again. I trained in every tactical and survival skill ever invented. Damien and I created King security and I have been searching for my dad's murderer ever since. One day I will find him, and I will put a bullet in his head."

Having never had this conversation with anyone before, it is remarkably easy. Chloe is extremely understanding and is surprisingly apologetic for taking the 'huff' with me, as she put it. She's been doing some research regarding her own nightmares and has some interesting suggestions that might help us both. "It's worth a try." She insists.

After breakfast, I drive us to the supermarket. Chloe talks non-stop the whole way around about the different ways we can help our night terrors. Some I'm on board with, others, like talking to a shrink, I'm definitely not up for.

Walking around the store I become infuriated. Men stop and stare as Chloe walks passed them. Even men with their partners take a second look. Jealousy rips through me. Chloe is oblivious to the attention she receives. The idea of insisting Chloe wears another style of clothing comes to mind. Maybe baggy trousers and a big jumper with a beanie hat? Huh! I laugh to myself, imagining Chloe's reaction if I was to suggest this. It probably wouldn't make much difference anyway. Her beauty would still shine through. I will just have to get used to it I suppose.

When we get home, I unpack the shopping looking forward to her reaction.

Chloe

"So, what were these 'essentials' we so desperately needed to get today then?" I ask as I root through the shopping Josh is trying to put away.

"Well, I noticed you were running low on Nutella" Very thoughtful and observant of him. "And then I also noticed we didn't have any of this." Josh pulls out a tub of cookie dough ice cream and places it next to the Nutella. I'm confused. Cookie dough is my favourite flavour of ice cream, but I don't remember telling that to Josh. It's also part of a Fantasy I have, that along with Nutella and a very naked Josh. The thought of this makes me smile.

Hold on a minute. Josh is looking extremely smug, standing there watching me. He now has the Nutella and ice cream in each hand doing a silly dance. I laugh and giggle at the sight.

He obviously knows somehow?

I know Bella wouldn't have told him.

Knowing Damien he probably had our table bugged.

I feel my face flush in a blush. It's unusual for me to get embarrassed.

"Well, by the look on your face big guy, I'm guessing you know what I'd like to do with those?" Josh's grin gets wider.

"So what you waiting for? Get that fit ass upstairs and take them with you!"

Josh looks surprised by my request, But he doesn't argue.

"Yes ma'am. You don't have to ask me twice." He turns and dashes upstairs. I grab some spoons and follow him up.

Chapter 7

Chloe

"On your back handsome." Having already removed his clothes, Josh follows my instructions and lies on the bed. He has an excited smirk across his face. I stand at the side of him and start to undress. Josh reaches out. I smack his hand away. "No touching. This is my fantasy remember." Josh puts his hands behind his head and watches my every move. I take my time undressing, enjoying watching the incredible man before me grow harder by second. Once I'm undressed, I straddle him on the bed. I rub myself gently up and down his length while watching Josh's eyes darken in colour. Again, Josh tries to touch me, I jump off him and cross the room.

"Hey, where you going?" I pull the belt off my dress gown and return to the bed. Josh looks at me in confusion.

"You're not playing like a good boy Josh. Give me your hands."

"No Clo. That's not happening." I put on my sad face and start to put my dressing gown on.

"Ggrrahh! Ok, ok!" Josh puts his hands above his head against the metal spindle headboard. I tie the belt around his wrists and loop it through the headboard. Give it a good pull so its extra tight. Now there will be no more interruptions.

Dipping my finger in the Nutella I watch Josh's breathing quicken as he observes my movements. I place my chocolate covered finger in my mouth and suck provocatively. I spread his legs and kneel in between them. With Nutella on my fingers, I stroke down his chiselled chest. Drawing along the outline of his muscular stomach. Admiring the beautiful man before me I lick my lips and straddle him, placing our throbbing intermit parts together. Josh bucks his hips trying to get inside me.

"Ah, ah, ahh…. be patient babe." I smile pushing myself against him to give that little bit of relief. I now follow my chocolate trail with my tongue. The mixture of chocolate, hazelnut and the deliciousness of Josh ignites all of my taste buds. The noises from Josh and sounds of his breathing encourage my excitement, I can't get enough of him. Once I have enjoyed all the Nutella, I reach for the ice cream. I put a large spoonful in my mouth and then suck on his nipple. Josh gasps and groans at the sensation. Wow. I feel so elated to be in control and making this amazing man beneath me make these incredible sounds. I Chloe Karen am making this man experience pure pleasure. Once I have treated both nipples to an experience they'll never forget, I move down to his crotch. With another large spoon of ice cream I take him in my mouth and devour him like the deliciousness he is. "CLO !" Josh growls as he explodes in my mouth. Our eyes hold each other's. I feel so proud and honoured to see, and be responsible for the look that is currently on Josh's face.

"Oh Clo." Josh breathlessly says trying to move his arms to touch me. "Untie me."

"I've not finished with you yet." Getting the tub of ice cream and the spoon I place his clean length inside me. "Hhhhhmmmm." I say in appreciation, and I feel him begin to harden again. Giving Josh a couple of minutes to recuperate I feed us both ice cream, cleaning any bits that spill from his mouth with my tongue. When I cannot wait any longer and Josh's hips buck to push himself deeper, I begin to ride him as he deserves. I'm so turned on. I feel so sexy and confident. I'm moving about like some kind of porn star and I feel incredible! When I can't hold out anymore, I press my face against Josh's and see relief in his eyes, he obviously has also been holding out as long as he could. We both lose control making synchronised love noises.

We lie in an embrace of sweating, adored bodies. "That was even better than my fantasy."

"I.... I can't even put that into words Clo." I giggle and get up to open the window, it's so hot and sweaty in here I need some air. *Whit woo* Josh wolf whistles at me as I walk across the room. It makes me smile.

Once the window is open, I hear a commotion outside. There's panicked shouting. I look out to see a man on the beach shouting frantically and pointing into the sea. It takes me a minute or so to see what he's point at. The sea looks really calm and there's nothing obviously untoward. But then I see it. A boy's head surfaces the water. It then disappears again only to resurface a few seconds later further out to sea. "Oh my god it's an undercurrent!"

"What ?! What's going on Clo ? Untie me now!" I don't hear what Josh's saying as my attention is focused on situation in front of me. The man is shouting the boy's name "TYLER !!!" My heart pangs. I cannot let another Tyler die in front of me. I throw on my underwear and top. I run down the stairs and out of the cottage as fast as my legs can carry me. I ignore the furious shouting from Josh. I haven't time to untie him, plus I know he would stop me swimming out to save him. That boy is exhausted. He's swimming against the current in panic. I have swum a lot in open water, I'm his best, well only chance. I run into the water as fast I can, then front crawl to the boy letting the current take me along with it to preserve my energy. The intervals in which the boy, Tyler, takes to resurface seem to last longer. Time seems to stand still while I swim but eventually, I reach him. His body is life less. I try to wake him but it's no use and we are being pushed further out to sea. Looks like I got here just in time, I hope. In the distance I hear an almighty roar from Josh. "CHLOE!" Oh dear. He's going to be soooo mad with me. I have no time to think about that now. I wrap am arm under Tylers and over his chest, I swim to the right, parallel to the shore. Holding on to him with one arm, I pull as hard as I can with the other. We don't move very far. It takes about 10 strokes of my arm and furious kicks of my legs just to move a few inches. But at least we aren't moving further out to sea, and we are moving in the right direction. From my bedroom window it only seemed metres to the end of the undercurrent, but here it seems much further. I push my body to the limit. I think of Tyler whose life had only just started really when it got taken away. I will not let this be the end of this boy's life. My mind switches into adrenaline power mode. I robotically move, I have no idea how long for, when suddenly everything seems incredibly easy, and we are moving at speed. It's then I hear my name. I look to the right and see Josh running into the sea towards us. He soon approaches, he grips the boy and I, and pulls us to land. When he can stand, he throws myself and Tyler over each one of his shoulders and carry's us to shore. My body falls limp over him in exhaustion. Once on the sand, the boy's father takes the boy from Josh and paramedics surround him. Josh then sits and puts me on to his lap, cradling me like a baby. Kissing my head he says to me.

"Don't you ever do that to me again. You hear me. Don't you ever do that to me again." Josh squeezes and rocks me, covering my head in kisses.

A paramedic comes over to check on me. "I'm fine. Really. How's the boy doing?"

"He's taken in a lot of water, and he's suffering from exhaustion. But he's alive, and that's thanks to you." At that moment Tyler's father falls to his knees in front of us.

"Thank you. From the bottom of my heart thank you. I'm so sorry. I panicked. I cannot swim. Thank you." The man completely breaks down. I break away from Josh and we both put an arm around him. "You did the best thing sir. You called for help. If you had entered the water, you both would have died. You saved your son sir. You did a good job." The man looks at Josh grateful for his words, even if he doesn't believe them. And I fall a little bit more in love with my wonderful man.

I let the paramedics give me a quick check over and Josh speaks to the coast guard. He's giving him a telling off actually. I laugh out loud which makes everyone stop and look at me. Josh has been talking with hands as usual and half of my dressing gown belt still hangs from his wrist. Josh looks at me confused with my laugh until he follows my line of sight. Realising himself what he has tied to his wrist, I think I see him blush for the first time. Smirking Josh mouths to me…

"I'll get you back for this."

Once the commotion on the beach disperses, Josh carry's me back to the cottage, despite my protest. "Oh no little lady. You do as I say from now on. I never want to go through what I experienced today, ever, ever again. Now I'm going to run you a hot bath and you will relax in there while I make us something to eat." Josh treats me like a delicate queen all night and I actually enjoy it. I completely let myself go and appreciate this hunk of a man taking care of me. I fall asleep in his arms feeling happy and content.

Josh

I can't get over yesterday. One minute I'm literally having the best moments of my life, the next I'm living my worst nightmare. Being tied to that bed and not being able to get to Chloe filled me with the most incredible heart aching rage. It took me what felt like hours but was probably only minutes to snap that dam dressing gown belt. That reminds me I need to fix the headboard. Seeing Chloe in that under current made me all sorts of crazy. I wanted to run in and hold her and pull her out. But I knew their best chance would be for her to do it by herself. The hardest thing I've ever had to do. Stand, watch and pray. Thankfully she's ok and she saved that lad's life. Chloe is one incredible woman. Today I'm taking Chloe out on my dad's old boat. I haven't seen it since my dad was alive, I'm looking forward to showing it to Chloe.

"So what are we doing today ? Fancy a swim in the sea?" Chloe jokes. I don't find it funny.

"Today and for the foreseeable, you will do exactly as your told." Chloe bites her toast and gives me a look I read as 'In your dreams.' I've got my work cut out with her.

"I'd like to see my dad's boat. Hopefully take it out and do some fishing. It's been in the boat yard for years so I'm not sure what condition it's going to be in. I have made sure it's been looked after, but you never know."

"I'm sure it's perfect Josh. Wow, I can't believe you have a boat. I can't wait to see it."

"It's just a fishing boat, not a fancy yacht, don't get too excited."

We get to the boat yard and a guy takes us to my dads boat. He pulls the cover off and I'm surprised to see how good she looks. The name Mary, after my mother, is written in black down the side. Looking as perfect as the day it was painted. My dad named it so that even when it was just the two of us having dad and lad time, my mum would be with us too. Memories come flooding back to me and I'm excited to get in it and out in the sea. "Give me a couple of hours and I'll get her in the marina for you. She's a beauty, shame to have her locked up in here. She belongs on the sea."

While we wait I take Chloe for a walk along the marina and show her where the best spots for crabbing are. I get us a bucket, a line, a net and some bacon for bait from the shop and we find a spot in between all the kids. "I've never heard of such a thing, fishing yes but not crabbing." Chloe laughs, which is music to my ears. I show Chloe how to tie the bait on the line and explain that the crabs are usually right at the bottom on some rocks or against the wall. Chloe is soon enthralled in the challenge. "Yey !!! That's seven! Aww look at them Josh, I've never seen a crab up close before. I really like them." The bucket is pretty full now. Chloe's caught seven large crabs as well as couple of little fish and shrimp. I've thoroughly enjoyed watching her getting excited over this. Maybe this is how my dad felt when he used to bring me here. On our walk back to the marina I stop at one of the food huts along the seafront. They're selling all kinds of seafood and shellfish. Chloe admits she's never had cockles or winkles. I'll soon change that. I get a portion of each along with some oysters, she liked those the other night, and we sit on a bench looking out to sea. "They're actually pretty good. I think the oysters are my favourite though with the vinegar on, but I like the cockles and winkles too." The way Chloe says cockles and winkles makes d**k stir. God I'm a sick man. We sit looking out to sea, watching and listening to the crashing waves and breathing in the salty air. Chloe takes my hand. "Thank you for bringing me here." I give her hand a squeeze and stand before that extra beat in my chest continues. I've never had the strength to come back here, but when I needed to get Chloe somewhere safe, I knew I had to return.

"Come on, Mary should be ready for us now." We grab some food and drink supplies from the shop and walk back.

Chapter 8

Josh

As soon as the marina is in sight, I see Mary. She looks incredible. Just like the first time dad and I set sail.

"Wow it's so fancy Josh. Look at all these buttons. I thought a boat just had a steering wheel and an on and off switch." Chloe's wandering around the cabin messing with everything. She is pretty awesome. No expense was spared when dad bought the boat new. She's years old now so very dated but still as immaculate as day one.

"You ready?" I say as I put the 'Captains Mate' hat on Chloe's head, the hat I used to wear. I guess I'm the 'Captain' now, I think as I put on my dad's hat.

We set sail out to sea, it's a beautiful sunny day and the sea is calm. Perfect for my first trip out with Chloe. We sail down the coast for a few miles until I find one of the spots I recognise. In the corner of my eye, I see Chloe removing her vest top. She is out on the stern of the boat and has my full attention now. As her arms lift up to pull it over her head, her breasts rise as she does, and then fall as she lowers them. I'm mesmerised by their perfect pear shapes. She's wearing a black bikini top which leaves little to the imagination.

"See something you like Captain?" Oh, do, I! I'm over there before she can finish that sentence. My lips meet hers and she's as hungry for me as I am for her. My hands roam down to her ass, she lifts herself and wraps her legs around my waist. We are pretty far out to sea, but I don't want to risk anyone getting a glimpse of what's mine, so I carry her into the cabin. I sit in the captain's chair with Chloe's legs on either side of me. We continue kissing while undressing each other. Chloe lifts herself and holds me at her entrance. She slowly lowers herself down, as if savouring every moment and sensation. The expression on her face and the noises she makes are enough to make me blow now. When I'm fully consumed by this beauty, Chloe really gets going. As much as I'm enjoying the ride, I need the control today. This is my boat and I am the Captain. I stand lifting Chloe and turning her round. "Bend over and put your hands out in front of you." Chloe obeys and lays her front on the control panel. "Spread your legs wider." Chloe lifts one of her legs and rests her foot on the steering wheel. I stand back for a second taking in the view. A gorgeous woman lay open and ready for me on my boat looking out into the sparkling ocean. I slide in and show Chloe just who is in charge today, "Captain Josh!"

We have a drink to cool off. I force myself to let go of Chloe and get out the fishing tackle. I can't get enough of her. Chloe seems really interested in what everything is and how it all works. She picks things up really easily too. I'm not sure if she's just putting all her enthusiasm on for me or whether she is actually enjoying it, but either way, I'm falling for her more than ever. Once our lines are prepared and cast, we relax in the sun and wait for the fish. Chloe talks of her childhood. She tells me about growing up with her grandma. They had a comfortable life but her grandma didn't drive and didn't like to fly or go on boats, so Chloe had never left the UK. I will show her the world one day.

"Me and Bella were going to go on a girl's holiday once to Tenerife but we both chickened out at the last minute. Bella gets anxious about everything, and I didn't have a clue about travelling abroad so we decided not to bother. I'll go somewhere one day." Chloe gets excited as her line starts to tug. I help reel it in. "It's a big one."

"It's a sea bass, good catch Chloe."

Once our food and drinks supplies have run out, we release the fish and dock the boat.

"Let's go out for food tonight. I fancy fish for some reason." Chloe giggles.

"What the lady wants, the lady shall get."

We are seated in the front of a seafood restaurant overlooking the sea. I can't take my eyes off Chloe. She's wearing a little black dress and her dark hair is in waves falling over her bare shoulders. The sun is setting over the sea and a candle flickers warm light across Chloe's skin. The sight is magnificent.

"Have a drink with me Josh."

"I'll have a tonic."

"Share a bottle of wine with me, please?"

"No. I don't drink when I'm working." That came out a lot more sternly than I meant. Chloe's expression shows the hurt my words created. I didn't mean how it sounded, I don't think of Chloe as work. I need to keep my wits about me and alcohol will jeopardise that, and I will not jeopardise Chloe's safety. I'm just about to apologise and explain when the waiter arrives to take our order.

We order a mixture of different seafood and Chloe gets herself a bottle of wine.

Chloe begins drinking the wine extremely fast, and I know it's because I've upset her. I take her hand across the table.

"I'm sorry Clo. You know that I don't think of you as work. I care about you so much, I cannot let anything happen to you. I need to be on top form twenty-four seven. I can't lose you, Clo, do you hear me?" She nods, picks up her glass, then downs the rest of the wine.

We enjoy the rest of the evening, talking and laughing about our day. But I still feel Clo has closed off. I could kick myself for what I said earlier. I've just got her to let her guard down and now she's put some of those walls back up.

After a trip to the gents' room, I find a waiter sat in my seat filling up Chloe's wine glass and saying something that has Chloe in fits of giggles. My blood boils. How F**king dare he. Neither of them notices me approach until I am stood directly behind the waiter. Chloe eyes meet mine, the laugher disappears from her face as she notices my annoyance. The waiter continues to talk in spite of my presence. I take the back of my chair and pull it out from under him. The waiter falls on the floor.

"You are in my seat." I say as he scrambles to feet. I wait for him to scuttle off into the kitchen before I sit down. Chloe has a smirk across her face. She does this on purpose, I am sure of it.

"Do you remember what I said to you before our first time?"

"Yes."

"Complete fidelity."

"Yes, I remember."

"Good, because if you flirt with him again, I will take you right now and show everyone who you belong to."

Chloe raises one eye brow, and for a moment I think she might test my threat.

Bring it on.

But she thinks better of it. A good job really, we are supposed to be keeping a low profile. Without taking her eyes off me she downs the last bit of her wine.

"Let's go big boy."

Chloe's a little tipsy on our walk back. We walk along the beach paddling our feet in the waves as they crash over the sand.

"I've just had the best idea, let's go skinny dipping." Chloe starts pulling her dress up over her body.

"Not a chance little lady!" I pick her up and throw her over my shoulder smacking her bum as I do. "You've caused me enough trouble already!" I carry a giggling Chloe back to our cottage and take her straight to bed.

"Lie with me, Josh." I snuggle in next to her. Today's fresh air and the wine have gone to her head, she is soon fast asleep. I lie and watch her as she sleeps until my arm is completely dead and I'm falling asleep myself. I gently roll her over and retire to my own room. I can feel sleep finally taking me and I don't want to be near Chloe when it does.

When I wake in the morning I feel a body next to me. Startled, I sit up to see Chloe laying completely still by my side. "Clo! Clo!" I shake her to get a response.

"What, what is?" thank goodness.

"What the hell are you doing in here?"

"Hey calm down Mr. I woke up in the night having had a nightmare and I couldn't get back to sleep."

"Are you sore anywhere? Did I hurt you?"

"No, Josh, I'm fine. Hey, Come here." Chloe wraps her arms around me and I start to relax a little. I didn't realise how fast my heart was beating until now. I couldn't bare it if I had hurt her.

"Look Josh. I sleep better when I'm next to you. You make me feel so safe I don't have nightmares. Maybe it is the same with you? Think about it. Whenever you have fallen asleep with me, You've never suffered from one." She is right come to think of it, but, it could all be a coincidence. I sit still for a while not saying anything, enjoying her holding me.

"You're so tense Josh, Lie on your front let me release some of the tension for you." I do as she says and enjoy those small magical fingers. They send tingles all the way through my body and end up in my d**k. When I'm about to explode I flip us both over and show her how good she makes me feel.

Chloe

The weeks go by so quickly, I'm loving every minute of being with Josh. He's changed me. He's made me let him in. Made me let him take care of me. If it wasn't for that crazy man after me, I would say I never want this to end. Josh has told me that Damien has made some good progress and that they know who the man is. It's only a matter of time now until they catch him. I just hope my relationship with Josh continues and it isn't just a holiday romance type thing.

I'm about to get in the shower but the water is still cold, I leave it running and go and find Josh to see if he can fix it. I hear voices coming from Josh's bedroom. I quietly stand outside his room and put my ear to his door. Josh is on the phone with Damien. I've always known that Josh spoke to Damien, but I have never heard him before, I often wondered when he did. I thought it must have been when I was asleep.

"Go head, Chloe's in the shower." That's what he

thinks. I listen as best I can but Josh must be walking around the room, so I only catch bits of the conversation.

"How is she now?"

"I'm waiting to speak to the doctor." They are talking about Bella. Something has happened to Bella. I strain to hear more, but I can't. I then hear Josh end the call and walk to the door. I dash back to the bathroom and quickly step under the shower, thankfully the water has warmed up a little. I cover my hair in shampoo just in time.

"Hello gorgeous, is there room for me in there?" Josh removes his clothes and joins me before I have time to protest. Not that I would.

I can't stop thinking about Bella. Is she ok? What has happened?

On our morning run I casually ask Josh if he has heard from Damien lately and how everyone back home is. He replies saying "Everything is fine, everyone is fine." He's not telling me so that I don't worry. Which means it must be serious.

If he won't tell me, I will find out for myself.

Later that day the perfect opportunity arises.

Chapter 9

Chloe

While in a restaurant I nip to the ladies' room. A group of girls are taking selfies in the mirror. When they leave, one of them has left their phone by the sink. I take it quickly and return to the toilet cubicle. Thankfully the passcode is to draw the code across the screen. Tilting the phone on its side I see the finger marks creating the shape of a triangle. After a couple of tries, as there are only so many ways to draw a triangle, I'm in. I dial Kingston manner as I can't remember Bella's mobile. Thankfully I have remembered it correctly. Penny answers "Good evening Kingston Manner, Penny speaking, how may I help you?"

"Penny, Its Chloe. I need to speak to Bella please and quickly."

"I'm sorry Chloe, Bella's not here. Her and Damien have gone away for a while, a holiday as such."

"Ahh ok, Is Bella ok Penny?"

"Of course. Damien will do all he can to protect Bella, you know that Chloe."

BANG "CHLOE?!"

"Got to go Penny, bye." I whisper. "Josh?.... I'm here I'm fine."

"You've been ages, what are you doing? Are you unwell?"

"No, I'm fine just go wait for me at the table."

"No, I'm waiting right here to see if you're alright. Open the door." I put the phone on top of the toilet and open the door, being careful not to fully open it, standing in the crack so he can't see passed me. Josh looks a little confused and is looking around suspiciously. "I've actually got a bad stomach. Can we go home now?" His suspicion turns to concern. Josh puts his arm around me

"Of course." As soon as we exit the toilet the selfie girls return looking for the phone I presume. Phew. That was a close one.

Bella is constantly on my mind. I keep going over the conversation with Penny. Something has happened. For the first time since we got here. I want to go home. I need to see Bella. I wish they'd hurry up and catch this guy.

I'm lay in the hammock on the front porch watching Josh fiddling with the cctv cameras.

"What are you doing Josh?"

"Checking for any lose connections."

"Oh right. Why?"

"Because this morning when we got up the Cameras and alarm system weren't on."

"So have you found anything wrong?"

"No, it's working perfectly now."

"Maybe you just forgot to set it last night?" Josh quickly turns to look at me. His stare is furious.

"I do not forget things Clo. Especially not

something as important as setting an alarm. I'll have one of the guys come check it again tomorrow."

Today I am feeling on edge. I think it must be the worry about Bella, it has brought back the reason as to why I am here. It's like my denial comfort bubble has popped and the seriousness of my situation has finally hit me.

Everything feels different today. Our usual run along the beach fills me with anxiety. It is the same route we normally take. I have Josh by my side, so I know I am safe, but I cannot shake this feeling. I feel vulnerable. I feel like I am being watched.

"Hey, what's up?" Josh asks as we get back to the cottage.

"Nothing, I'm fine." I give Josh my most convincing smile.

"MMM. How about we have a day on the sofa today? I can bring all the duvets down and we can snuggle up and watch that 'mates' programme you like?"

I laugh so hard.

"You mean 'Friends'?"

"Yeah, that's the one. The one you watch with Bella. I'll be a girl for the day. I will make us some popcorn and we can have pillow fights or whatever it is girls do?"

"That sounds amazing Josh. Thank you."

"If you're a good girl I might even let you have some ice cream and Nutella."

We spend the day snuggled up. We get all the

cushions off the sofa and make a bed on the floor. I introduce Josh to 'Friends' and he admits he really enjoys it. We eat pizza, popcorn, and chocolate like it's going out of fashion. We laugh and kiss and cuddle. It has been the best day.

"This is it for me you know Clo."

I look at Josh trying to read his expression. He is still facing the tele as if he's nervous.

"Me too." I can't believe we are saying these words.

"Look at me."

His eyes are full of emotion.

"When we get home. You'll move in with me."

I smile as a few weeks ago I would have protested at a man telling me what to do. But now. With Josh. He can boss me around however he wants.

"Ok."

Josh cups my face with both of his hands.

"I love you, Clo."

My heart bursts and my eyes fill with tears.

"I love you too Josh."

We make love into the early hours until we are completely exhausted. I am soon in a deep, contented sleep. That is.......

Until......

I wake to a hand over my mouth.

Chapter 10

"Shhhhh……..There's someone in the house."
Josh's mouth is to my ear.

Panic sets in and I can hear my heart beating.

We lie still, trying to breathe quietly so we can listen.

I don't hear anything, but Josh is tense and on high alert. Even in the darkness, I can see his eyes scanning the room. I know what he is thinking. He always sleeps with a gun under his pillow. But the gun is upstairs on his bed. I know there's one strapped to the underneath of the kitchen table but that's at the other side of the room.

After a few minutes, I hear it. The sound of footsteps squeaking on the wooden floors. My breathing becomes uncontrollable. My heart is racing. My body begins to shake. They are getting nearer and nearer. The footsteps stop about a meter away from us. If I was to look in that direction, I would be able to see them. But I don't, I am paralysed in fear.

"Love you Clo." Josh jumps out of bed with such a force. I can hear him fighting with another man, but I can't look.

I close my eyes tight and pray for it to be over.

There's shouting and growling.

"GET OUT CLO!" I can hear Josh shouting me, but I am frozen, I can't even move my head.

BANG

Josh's body lands at the side of me.

Everything goes quiet.

I am now brought out of my paralysis. I sit up to see Josh on the edge of our make-shift bed. The gun man stood over him. It's him. The guy that killed Tyler, I'd recognise those evil eyes anywhere. He has found us.

Looking very pleased with himself he lifts his gun to me. With a mighty growl, Josh launches himself off the floor and over the top off me. *BANG*

"I..love you….so much …Clo." I wrap my arms around him.

"Don't you dare leave me Josh. Don't you dare." I feel my stomach becoming warm and wet with his blood. Josh's body becomes limp. "No! No! No!" I cry shaking him, but he's unresponsive.

"Well, well, well. I finally found you. You know, I almost gave up. But I knew you would slip up eventually." He voice is smug and makes my blood boil. "A call was made to your best friend's home from this area, so I thought I would come and check it out. And here you are. You are no match for me little girl. Even your bodyguard boyfriend couldn't protect you."

I move out from under Josh. I catch sight of myself covered in blood. Physically feeling my heart break, I no longer have any concern for myself. I cannot live without him. Adrenaline fills me, I run towards the gunman. I punch him in the face with all the force I can muster. He drops to the floor in a daze. But it doesn't last for long. Laughing, he gets to his feet.

"I'm going to enjoy this." I turn to run out of the cottage, but he grabs me by hair. I am thrown into the wall, my face smashing against a mirror. It breaks slicing the skin on my forehead. I'm spun around and met with a kick to the stomach. It takes my breath away. He lets go of my hair and I drop to the floor on all fours. Still unable to breathe I receive a forceful boot to the temple. I feel a crack to my scull and a piercing ring bellows in my ears. I stay down praying for it to be over. Surely another couple of kicks like that and I'll be done. He paces around me.

"I have waited so long for this." Another boot batters my face. The ringing in my ears is excruciating.

"STOP!" A voice I don't recognise fills the room.

I am lifted off the floor and sat on a chair. My body is limp, I slump back into it. A light is turned on visualising the horrific scene I am in. Josh is lay lifeless in our bed of cushions. The once white bedding is now dark red. My heart is broken.

"WHAT THE HELL ARE YOU DOING HERE?!"

"You need to stop this Cain! She is your sister!"

I am in and out of consciousness. I am not sure if I have heard him correctly. I look up to a man I vaguely recognise. He wets a towel in the sink and sits down in front of me.

"May I?" I don't respond. I was hoping this nightmare would be over by now. He dabs and cleans my face. I do not understand what is going on. I don't have the energy to ask. All I can do is look at my lifeless man on the floor. I no longer care about anything. I am numb.

"You are so beautiful. Just like your mother."

"Hold on a minute. What the hell is going on here? She, is a dead woman, and how the F**K did you find me?"

The man stands furious. "YOU WILL NOT LAY ANOTHER FINGER ON HER!" The man has an American accent. I remember now where I know him from. I met him in the King security building. He had a meeting with Josh that day I spoke to the police.

"Mr Graves?" the name comes out of me in a whisper.

"Yes darling that's me." Mr Graves sits down again. He has a concerned look on his face.

"Chloe, let me introduce my son. Cain. I am sorry for the hurt he has caused you. I have tried to stop him." I now have a name to put to the evil face. Cain lights a cigarette and blows the smoke in our direction.

"You've got five minutes to explain yourself, then I will be putting a bullet in her head."

Mr Graves glares at him.

"Thirty years ago, I fell in love with the most beautiful woman in the world. She loved me unconditionally. But I was a bad man. I treated her terribly."

He continues to talk but my ears switch off and I'm lost in thoughts of my mother. I don't have any real memories of her. Well, I don't think I do. Smells sometimes remind me of her, certain sweets or fabric softeners. Maybe these are memories of how she smelt. I was six months old when she died. It broke my grandparent's hearts. My grandpa never recovered, and he passed away when I was about seven. My grandma always said "There will always be something good to come out of what's bad, sometimes you just need to look very hard to find it." Grandma always said that in the situation of losing my mother, the good, was me. That she got to have cuddles with me every day. There were always lots of photographs of my mum around the house. She was very beautiful. People always say I look just like her.

I asked my grandma multiple times about my father, but she always said she knew nothing about him. Not even his name. Grandma told me mum had gone off the rails a bit before becoming pregnant. That my grandparents hadn't seen her months until one day she turned up pregnant with me. They had asked her who the father was, but she said he didn't want anything to do with us, so they never pushed. My grandma always thought they would find out eventually, but when she passed there was no way to find out.

"And so, when I saw you that day, I just knew you

were my daughter. You look the spitting image of your mother. When you said your middle name was Karen after your mother, I was certain." Mr Graves continues. "I followed you and your friend to a restaurant, when you left, I took one of your glasses and had a DNA test done. It's a match. We are father and daughter." Mr Graves hands me a piece of paper, but I don't take it. I do not care who this man is. And why hasn't he rung an ambulance and the police? Cain stamps his cigarette out on the floor. He throws a chair across the room.

"I don't care who you are. I need to call an ambulance." I scream as I get up and walk over to Josh.

"Oh no you don't!" Cain grabs me and pushes me back into my seat.

"Leave her alone! Did you not hear what I just said?!"

"She is no sister of mine!"

Both men shout and argue with each other.

I switch off. I stare at my lifeless Josh. How can this be? How can I go from being the happiest I have been to my heart being ripped out of my chest? The men are now flighting. Cain beats his father until he can no longer stand. He then grabs me by my hair and puts me against the wall.

He stands back to look at me.

"Finally." With a smirk on his face, he lifts his gun to me. I close my eyes.

I feel a heaviness in my chest. It forces my back against the wall. I then slide down to the floor.

Still, with my eyes closed, I hear Cain.

"F**K!!!!!"

I open my eyes to see Mr Graves lay across me. Cain storms over to me and pushes the barrel of the gun in between my eyes.

"No one can take the bullet for you now!"

Praying for it to be over, praying to be reunited with Josh, I stare into Cains eyes. They are dark and evil.

BANG

A dark red spot appears in the middle of Cain's forehead.

The expression on his face disappears. Blood begins to pour from the dark round hole.

His body drops to the floor in a heap. My heart picks up as look for my hero. Is it Josh? Is he still alive? Is he ok? I look around the room and see my saviour in the doorway.

My heart sinks. It's not Josh. Its Damien.

My ears are ringing, and my eyes are a blur. Paramedics fill the cottage. People are speaking to me, but I can't tell what they are saying to me. I am strapped to a chair and wheeled out to the ambulance.

As I pass Damien, I hear the paramedics talking to him.

"I'm sorry sir. He's gone."

Chapter 11

*Three months earlier. The day of
the youth centre shooting.*

Damien

Having dropped Bella off at home I enter the youth centre. I show my I.D and speak to one of the detectives whom I have met many times.

"We have one deceased 16 year old male in here." We stand at the door. I see the boy lying on the ground surrounded by his blood. Police forensics have arrived and started taking pictures. The scene makes my blood run cold. What a traumatic experience the people in this room would have encountered. I move down the hall having seen enough.

"There are another two casualties, again teenage males, with gunshot wounds to their legs. They have been taken to the hospital by the paramedics, thankfully their injuries aren't life-threatening. Everyone else is congregated in the games room. We are waiting for 'appropriate adults' to arrive for the minors and then we can take statements. As of yet we don't have much to go on for the suspect, unfortunately."

The games room is full of distraught teenagers. Their families are starting to arrive now, the room gets louder with emotion. I see Josh and make my way over to him.

"The detective's brought me up to speed. How's Chloe?"

"She's being incredibly strong. Making sure everyone else is ok. I haven't had chance to speak to her properly yet." We both watch her as she comforts the teenagers. She hugs them, listens to them and even makes them smile. They obviously think a lot of her. A police officer walks over to Chloe and pulls her away from the girl she is currently speaking to.

"I'm going over there." Josh joins Chloe and her face fills with relief when she sees him at her side.

I call Bella to let her know that Chloe is safe and well.

Once we are back at home, we leave the girls together and Josh and I go over today's events.

"The CCTV on that building is atrocious. It's like something from the 1950's, absolutely useless. Good job Chloe's on the ball and recorded it."

"Yeah, she's an incredible woman."

"She's putting on a brave face, but it will hit her sooner or later."

"I know, I will keep an eye on her." I have no doubt he will.

"I think it will be a good idea to arrange some protection until the gunman is found. We don't know who he is yet, or if he is working for someone. Based on what I heard today, Chloe is the most reliable witness, and she is the one who got him on film. We need to keep an eye on her at all times."

"She will be my priority. I will speak to a couple of the guys in the morning and make sure we have all areas covered."

We go and check on the girls.

"We are going for a swim."

"We will come with you." Josh nudges me. I didn't really fancy a swim but I'll get to see my Bella in her bikini. I will also observe how she is with Chloe. Bella's not been herself lately. She has assured me she is fine but there is something I cannot put my finger on.

After doing some lengths of the pool, the girls go into the steam room.

"Has Chloe said anything to you about Bella?"

"No. Like what?"

"There's something not right, yet she is adamant she is fine."

"Mate, women are a complicated luxury. It's not our job to work them out. Only to be there when they need us. Plus, Chloe doesn't speak to me about things like that. We have a friendly relationship. Nothing more."

I nod, not wanting to pry.

When we retire to bed, I start to massage Bella's

shoulders. She is facing the opposite way, so I snuggle in behind her and breathe in her scent. I still can't get enough of her. Pressing my hard length in between her bum cheeks I wrap my arms around her and kiss her neck.

"Not tonight Damien, I'm tired."

What?! I roll back in utter shock and disappointment. Are we really here already? I obviously don't expect to have Bella whenever I wish but I don't even get a kiss or a cuddle?

I turn back toward her, leaning up on my elbow. I stroke the back of her head.

"Hey, Bella. What's up?" Bella slowly turns around.

"What's up?? I have turned you down, so you think there must be something up? There's nothing 'up' Damien. I'm just tired." Bella pulls the covers up to her neck and rolls over to the far side of the bed.

There's definitely something wrong. Bella has never spoken to me like that before. I'm angry because I know there is something she is not telling me. I can read people well, especially Bella. With anyone else, I would force it out of them, but with Bella, I cannot do that. I will let her calm down and speak to her tomorrow.

With gritted teeth, I wish her good night. I struggle to sleep due to my mind analysing every movement and conversation Bella has had recently. I know Bella is extremely upset over what has happened to Chloe. I also know tonight should have been a surprise birthday party for me, so she will be disappointed that didn't work out. But it isn't any of those things.

After hours of scrutinization, I realise the obvious. "I'm sorry I snapped at you last night Damien, I was very upset and worried for Chloe. I will give you lots of attention tonight I promise."

"No need to apologise my Bella." I take her in my arms and kiss her gently but passionately.

"We'd better get up. We must give Chloe a lift and I have some errands to run if you don't mind driving me?"

"Of course."

Bella

I feel terrible. I'm in the car with Damien, sweating, because I am trying to stop myself from being sick. Damien is talking to me and all I can do is nod or make mumbling sounds. He seems really concerned about me. I really snapped at him last night and I feel awful for it, but I need to explain all this when I am feeling one hundred percent, which right now, I am not.

I'm having lunch with Chloe today, she will cheer me up, although it should be me cheering her up after what happened yesterday. Hopefully I will feel better later, and I will tell Damien he is going to be a father. Oh gosh, my stomach flipped. I really hope he is happy. We have talked about having a family together and said we would like to start soon, but this is very soon. Damien had said he wanted us to be married first, so I hope he isn't disappointed.

My lunch with Chloe is just what I need. She knew I was pregnant without me even telling her. I am so lucky to have someone so close to me.

We laugh and talk for hours. Chloe is her usual bubbly self, although I can see through it. I know that yesterday has affected her, and she is putting a brave face on for me. I wish she didn't feel like she needed to do that. Chloe has always been there for me. I wouldn't be who I am today if it wasn't for her, but I just wish for once she would let me look after her. Chloe has always acted like my big sister and now I want to repay the favour. She's so brave and strong, but it can't be good keeping everything bottled up. A problem shared is a problem halved, my mum always says. I try and speak about it, but Chloe just brushes it off. If there's one thing I know about Chloe, it's that if she doesn't want to do something, then she won't and there is no persuading her otherwise. I won't be giving up though.

We talk about her and Josh, they are so into each other but neither of them can see it. It will happen between them I know it.

Chloe fills me with excitement and confidence about the baby. I can't wait to get home and tell Damien now. And it looks like that will be sooner than I thought. Damien has just walked in, but he doesn't look happy.

"Hey sweetheart, are you ok?" I ask Damien, concerned by the look on his face.

"Not really." Damien replies as he quickly ushers

me out of the restaurant and into the car.

"What's wrong?"

"We will discuss it when we get home."

Sadness fills me. Has he found out about the baby? Is he upset with me for letting this happen? Oh no, has this made him rethink our relationship? Panic runs through me, I can't breathe. I am having a panic attack.

"Stop the car!"

"What?!"

"Stop the car I am going to be sick." Damien pulls over and I am out of the car before it comes to a stop. I dash to a bush by the side of the road. I am just in time as my lunch and the litre of water I have demolished this afternoon removes themselves from my stomach.

Damien sweeps the hair back from the sides of my face and holds my hair until I'm done. Rubbing my back he asks "How are you feeling?" I stand and nod, not sure if I can speak yet. Damien hands me a tissue and guides me over to a bench a couple of feet further down.

"You should have told me, Bella." Damien whispers as he kisses the top of my head helping me to sit down. I push the hair out of my face and rub my eyes, when I open them, they're met with Damien's. His face level with mine. I notice he is kneeling in front of me.

"From that first moment I laid eyes on you Bella, I knew you were meant for me. Your beauty dazzled me, and your soul spoke to mine. My heart now beats for yours. I don't ever want to live without. I am eternally grateful that I found you." Damien reaches into his pocket and pulls out a red velvet box. Opening it to reveal a twinkling diamond on a golden band, he takes my hand in his.

"Bella White, will you do me the greatest honour and agree to become my wife?"

Feeling overwhelmed I throw my arms around him and sob into his shoulder. He picks me up and twirls us around.

"Is this a, yes?" Damien chuckles.

"Yes, It's a Yes!"

Forgetting that I have just been sick Damien kisses me with one of his kisses that go straight to my heart.

"I love you, Bella White, soon to-be Mrs King."

"I love you too."

Damien places the ring on my finger and it fits perfectly.

"I hope you like it, it reminded me of you, dainty and full of sparkle."

"I love it, I really do." The thin gold band feels wonderful around my finger. I twist and turn my hand to see the glimmers and sparkles from the round diamond set in the centre. I can't believe it.

It's a lovely sunny day so we go for a little walk hand in hand. We stroll through a field which is full of daisies.

"So come on Bella, please put me out of my misery. I think I know but I need to hear it from you."

I stop and take his face in my hands. Staring into

those gorgeous deep eyes I tell him.

"Damien King, my fiancé. You are going to be a father. We are pregnant."

Damien's mouth twitches and for a second a glaze fills his eyes, but he soon blinks it away and takes a deep breath which catches as he does. Picking me up for the second time today, he spins us around and kisses me until he sits us down in daisies with me on his lap.

"When did you find out? Why didn't you tell me straight away." Damien looks saddened in his question.

"I only found out the day before yesterday. I wanted to tell you straight away but then I thought I'd tell you on your birthday seeing as it was only a day away. It was silly of me I'm sorry I just wanted it to be perfect." Damien smiles and gives me a squeeze.

"It would always have been perfect, but I understand. I too have been waiting for that 'perfect' time to propose. My plan was my birthday also. It just goes to show, as long as we are together, the where and when really doesn't matter."

Damien is right. We spend the next hour making daisy chains, laughing, kissing and cuddling. It couldn't have been more perfect.

That evening Damien makes love to me in the most gentlest and affectionate way. Every nerve of my body feels the love between us. I thought the love we shared couldn't have gotten any stronger, but it has. We now have an unbreakable bond. Our child.

I saw Damien slyly googling whether having intercourse could harm a pregnancy, so I know the reason behind Damien's more cautious lovemaking. Even though he would have seen there is no risk, he still wants to protect us both.

"I will arrange a doctor's appointment and early scan for first thing tomorrow morning. I love you my Bella." He says as he kisses my head and I drift off into a content and exhausted sleep.

"Good morning, Mr King. Please both of you come in and take a seat."

"Good morning, Dr Jones, thank you for seeing us at such short notice. This is Bella, my fiancé"

Wow, I love hearing him call me that.

The appointment goes well, it turns out I am much farther along than I first thought. I am already twelve weeks. I watch Damien's expression upon hearing this news, his face fills with worry as he relives the last 12 weeks in his mind, obviously worrying about what we may have done. There's no need to worry though, Dr Jones gives both me and the baby a strong bill of health. The baby has a strong heartbeat is a good size and looks perfect. After Damien has fully interrogated poor Dr Jones we leave with our hearts full of emotion.

"I am taking you to lunch to celebrate."

Damien takes me to a beautiful high-rise restaurant with a fantastic view over the river Thames and the London skyline. We are of course seated at the table with the best view in the restaurant even though the place is booked solid for the next six months.

Picking up the menu Damien starts to recite the options I have, as many of them contain various ingredients which aren't advisable to eat while pregnant. Chloe would hate anyone telling her what she should or shouldn't eat, but I like it. I love how Damien looks after me, and after all, it is his baby too.

Knowing everything is ok with the baby is such a relief. We start to discuss and imagine what the little mini us will be like.

"Would you like to find out the sex of the baby?"

"I think I would enjoy a surprise, but if you would prefer to know my Bella, then that is what we shall do." He makes me so happy.

I look out and watch the world passing by feeling so grateful to be happy. I then think of Chloe and what she must be going through. Hopefully, this baby will cheer her up and give her something to focus on.

"What's wrong Bella?"

"I am just thinking of Chloe, I hope she will be ok."

"She will. Josh and I will make sure of it."

Just then Damien's phone rings. He answers and I know it is serious.

"We need to leave."

Chapter 12

Damien

Bella and I stand at the front door waiting for Josh and Chloe's arrival. The gunman from the youth centre had found Chloe, thank fully Josh rescued her.

The last few day's events are unbelievable. Chloe's life is in danger. We need to catch this bast**d. He is putting my fiancé and unborn child in danger as well as Chloe and I will not stand for it. The worry alone is harming enough, especially for Bella as she suffers greatly from anxiety.

When they arrive, I take Josh to see the medical team while Bella comforts Chloe.

"Ten of the guys are now on a warning for their foolish actions which did not help today's events. Gatherings with more than four members of staff at one time outside of work is now forbidden. I have HR adding it to their contracts. I am sorry I wasn't around Josh. How are you?"

"It's been a day of unavoidable situations. It is no one's fault." I hear the words spoken by Josh's mouth, but I can tell by his face, he doesn't believe them. He is blaming himself.

"Quite right, it is no one's fault other than that

crazy excuse for a man. What else have we got to go on? The police must have something?" I am usually more on the ball with incidents like this, but with everything that has gone on with Bella and the baby, my mind has been elsewhere.

"The police are coming here shortly to speak to us. We will find out then."

"I have a team with his description and all the information we know out there looking for him. They will be out 24/7 until he is caught. Dead or alive I have left the decision with them."

Josh nods, wincing with pain as the medics clean up his gunshot wound.

"She's not safe here Josh. You need to go into hiding. Just until he's caught."

"I've been thinking the same."

"Have you any idea where you could go?"

"Yeah. I do actually."

"Great. You must leave tonight. The girls won't be happy, but it's for the best."

Once we have seen Josh and Chloe on their way, I take Bella up to bed. She is exhausted and very emotional.

"What am I going to do without her Damien? I have never gone a day without speaking to Chloe."

"They'll be back before you know it." Bella lays her head on my chest and has a little sob.

"At least I'm at the salon tomorrow. Katie will be there, and I'm fully booked, from what I can remember. That will take my mind off it." I was hoping Bella would give up work now she is pregnant. Financially there is absolutely no need for Bella to ever work again, but I know hairdressing is more of her hobby. Although I would love to insist Bella starts her maternity leave immediately, I know that wouldn't be fair. Plus I think it may be a welcome distraction for a while, now Chloe has gone away. I will, of course, be working from my office at the salon.

"Good morning guys, how are you all?" I greet the team in the salon before I go to my office. Bella seems a lot happier and more relaxed now she is here.

"Let me know if you need anything Bella, I'll just be in my office." I kiss Bella on the head and settle at my desk. I have a lot to catch up on.

I'm busy on the phone when Mike the salon security guard enters. He stands at my desk waiting for me to finish. It must be important, so I swiftly close the conversation and end the call.

"Yes Mike, what can I do for you?"

"We have a problem boss. This has just been delivered to Bella." Mike hands me a card box addressed to my Bella. I open it to find a pair of eyes staring back at me. A pair of blood soaked animal eyes. I throw the box on my desk.

"F**K!!" He's right. We do have a problem.

"It's starting again boss. We just assumed that the deliveries to Bella the last time were from John or Pete. But it looks like they were from someone else."

"It does indeed."

This is the last thing we need. Who the devil could be sending these things to Bella. Who would want to hurt Bella now? Could it be related to the incident with Chloe? But this all started long before Chloe moved to London.

"No mention of this to Bella. Did she see you receive the parcel?"

"No boss, she didn't see anything arrive, she was busy with her client."

"Good, keep your wits about you Mike, go with your gut. Anything slightly off and I need to know about it."

"Understood."

Mike leaves my office and I stand and pace. I feel like putting my hand through the wall. I won't, as that will alert Bella and she will know there's an issue. Bella has enough to worry about. I will not let anyone hurt her. I will kill anyone who touches her. I will not lose her again.

I contact my team who trace the eyes back to a local delivery company. They were given the parcel and asked to deliver it as part of a practical joke. I spoke to the manager personally, and let's just say they won't be participating in any practical jokes in the future. Idiots. They gave a vague description of a male who paid with cash. I doubt it will lead anywhere. I pick up the phone to ring Josh and then remember I can't. We have a scheduled call tomorrow night on radio phones once they are settled. It makes me uneasy not being able to speak to him.

Josh and I have been friends since school. His father was murdered around the same time as Claire committed suicide. The traumas brought us even closer together. When we left education, we both needed to focus our anger on something positive, so we started King Security.

Bella

It's been a busy day in the salon. I am exhausted. I thought it would take my mind off things with Chloe, but it hasn't. I have spent today worrying about her and our baby. Damien has been at the salon all day working. He is trying to act normal, but I've seen him with Mike and I can tell he is worrying about me. I have a midwife appointment tonight.

On the drive over Damien seems distracted.

"Hey, is everything ok? Have you spoken to Josh? How's Chloe?"

"Everything is fine my Bella." Damien says as he brings my hand to his mouth and kisses it.

"Josh and Chloe are safe, and we will soon have the guy behind bars. All you need to concentrate on is yourself and that little baby of ours."

When we arrive at the clinic Damien's phone rings so I tell him to take the call. I go into the treatment room and the midwife takes my blood pressure and some bloods. She seems a little distracted, maybe she's having a bad day. That is until the door opens and my fiancé walks in. Damien pulls up the chair next to me and turns it slightly so he's facing me. He talks my hand and then looks at the midwife in confusion. She completely stopped talking mid-sentence.

"Continue." Damien instructs in his powerful way. "Yes, so as I was saying the morning sickness should continue to get better, but if you have any other symptoms you are worried about or any questions, anything at all you just ring me. I'll write my mobile number on the top of your pregnancy notes." The midwife has completely changed personality since Damien walked through the door. She's sat up straight, pushing her boobs out, fluttering her eye lashes and playing with her hair. Amusingly Damien hasn't even noticed. His eyes haven't left mine and he's holding my hand on his lap. The midwife finishes up and Damien's phone rings again, he excuses himself and leaves the room. I gather my things as the midwife catches my arm.

"Oh my god, you lucky thing. He is so hot! You're not married are you?" Before I can answer Damien returns to the room.

"We will be soon, not that it is any of your business. It is also myself that is the lucky one. I suggest you make sure on our next visit you act nothing but professional, or I shall be speaking to your superior." She looks as though she might cry. Oh well she deserves it. I follow my man back to the car admiring the gorgeous protective man he is. What I did to deserve him I will never know. But

I am forever grateful.

"What are you smiling at Bella?"

"Just you, I love you Damien."

"I love you too, and I know that look. Mmmmm."

"Yeah? Well hurry up and get me home fiancé."

"Oh no, I can't wait till we get home. Climb in."

Damien opens the back door of his Bentley. I smile excitedly and do as he says. The Bentley is extremely spacious and the back windows are completely blacked out. Damien slides in after me, he picks me up and places me on his lap. I turn and straddle him. I can already feel him hot, hard and ready for me.

"Aahhhh." I grown as I push myself against him. Damien has always made me horny but with these pregnancy hormones I'm ready to go every minute.

We kiss deeply, both as equally hungry for each other. Damien's hands are on my neck and bottom. Massaging and squeezing just as I like, melting me into him even more. I run my hands over his big shoulders and chest, then down to his large length I crave. I lift up as Damien releases himself and discards my panties in the process.

"Climb on my Bella. Let me in that heaven of yours." Damien growls like he's trying his best to hold on. I lift up guiding him in. I slowly slide down enjoying every inch and stretch. My breath catches as the euphoria becomes me. Once I'm as far as I can take him, Damien's eyes turn a darker shade of brown. He grabs my face and kisses me with such desire. His hands move to my hips taking my weight. Using his hips he grinds and pounds our intermit areas together. Massaging both of my sensitive spots. In and out simultaneously, sending tingles and shivers throughout my body. I'm there. My insides begin to contract, my legs begin to shake.

"Look at me Bella! I need to watch you."

I hold Damien's eyes as we both reach our climax. Heaven.

I relax into him, resting my head on his shoulder and kissing his now sweat glistened neck. He tastes all salty and manly, delicious.

"I love you my Bella, soon to be my wife."

"I love you too."

Driving out of the clinic car park we get a few stares. Although the windows are blacked out it doesn't take a rocket scientist to work out what we were doing. The rocking and noises coming from the car may have given us away. There was once a time where I would have been mortified, but with Damien, I feel like I can just be who I want to be.

"I'm thinking of reducing my hours at the salon. At least cutting down on my clients anyway. I'll probably still go to the salon, I can't just sit at home doing nothing. If I'm not on my feet all day, that should help with the tiredness."

"Bella, you know full well that if you're in the salon you will be constantly on your feet. You will end up doing clients that weren't booked in, because they are desperate for one reason or another and you won't be able to say no. Or one of the stylists will be running behind and you will help out. It just won't work Bella. You need to be out of the salon at home resting. To be honest I think you should start your maternity leave now."

"What? No. I can't just stop working. What will all my clients do? And the staff? No, I need to wind down so that when I go in to labour there won't be many clients let down."

"When you go into labour? Don't be ridiculous Bella, you will not be working until anywhere near your due date."

"Don't you tell me what to do! I will work until I see fit!" I wish I had never brought up the subject now. How dare he say I should give up work now. It is my business, my passion, what I have worked for all these years.

The rest of the drive home is in silence. We pull up at the house and I am out of the car before George or Damien can open my door. Honestly, he treats me like a delicate child sometimes. I go to our room and slam the door in temper.

I wish I could ring Chloe, I would tell her all about what Damien said and she would calm me down and give me some good advice. She would probably tell me Damien is only worrying about me and wants what is best. Dam! Why is he always right. Well not entirely. I will not be going on maternity leave any time soon and that's for sure.

I get out all the papers and leaflets I got from the midwife. I have a read through them to take my mind off things. It's beginning to feel so real now. I've just about calmed down when there's a knock at the door.

Chapter 13

Damien

I knock gently on our bedroom door.

"Come in." Good, at least she is speaking to me. I've left Bella for an hour to calm down. And for myself. I know I can't insist Bella starts her maternity leave yet, it is very early but I can insist she takes it easier. Working up until she is due will not be happening, but I expect she will change her own mind about that nearer the time.

"I'm sorry about earlier Bella, I just want to protect you and our baby. If I could wrap you up in cotton wool and keep us all in here until the baby is born, I would. But I cannot ask that of you. You have a life, and I will respect that. I do think we perhaps need a little compromise? If you're up to discussing it?"

Bella doesn't shout and tell me to leave, so I take a seat next to her on the bed.

"Ok, what are you thinking then Damien?"

"I think you were right earlier. You do need to reduce your hours. But I think when you're not working you should be at home relaxing."

"Hmmm, I agree. I would probably end up still working if I was in the salon. But I want to be at the salon for as long as possible. It won't be long until I won't be there at all. I'm going to decrease my appointment times, so that I'm not doing as many clients in one day. And I'm going to take a Thursday off so it breaks my week up. I'm not going to be sat at home doing nothing all day though. I have been going through the leaflets that the midwife gave us, and there's a few activities I fancy."

Well, I'm glad Bella's cutting back, albeit not as much as I'd like. I'm not sure about pregnancy activities however, unless I am able to attend too.

"What are these activities you speak about?" Bella hands me a pile of leaflets.

"There are all sorts. Some are for further down the line and mother and baby groups. I fancy the pregnancy yoga and aqua gym. The leaflet says it's good for relaxation as well as mental and physical health. There are classes on Thursday at the church hall."

"If that's what you would like to do, then that is what you shall do."

I pull Bella into a hug, kiss her head and breathe her sweetness in. I hate when we argue. I'll have to get in contact with the church hall and sort out the security. For now, I shall leave out the part that Bella will only be attending these activities with myself or one of my team. I don't want to upset her again tonight.

"Come down to the kitchen, I have made us some dinner."

Bella picks at her food, it's very unlike her. This

pregnancy is really affecting her. If it wasn't my baby causing all these changes to Bella's body I would resent it.

"I thought we could go to my parents this weekend and tell them the news? It's so hard not telling them when I speak to them over the phone, but I really want to see their reaction in person. They'll be so excited for us Damien."

Bella's is beaming again now and I'm very grateful. When she is happy, I am happy.

"Wonderful idea my Bella." I will rearrange a few things and work from there.

"Would you be able to rearrange your diary at the salon so we can make a long weekend of it?" Bella rolls her eyes and smiles.

"I suppose, but don't you think you can just tell me to cancel work and I will."

"I would never think such a thing."

"Good. I'm only doing it as it is a special occasion. Plus, I can't very well announce I'm pregnant and engaged to my parents and then leave the next day. My mum is going to want to go shopping and do some planning. Eeek! It's so exciting Damien."

This weekend away is a brilliant idea. I don't know why I haven't thought of it. It will get us a way from here, hopefully the gunman and the psychopath who is sending things to Bella will be resolved by the time we return, although I doubt it unfortunately.

"Ring your parents and make sure it is convenient. Then I'll make arrangements. We will stay in a hotel."

Bella speaks to her mum who insists we stay with them. I am perfectly comfortable staying in their home. It is lovely. It just means in an evening I will have to keep my hands to myself, so to speak. Or be extremely quiet. Neither option pleases me, but I'm sure I'll manage for one weekend.

"Dad wants to know if you'd like to play golf on Sunday?"

"Yes of course, I'd love to." Love is an incredibly strong word for what I actually feel about playing golf. I have been having a few lessons, just so I don't look a complete fool and show Bella's father up on the golf course. But I really am a typical 'all the gear, no idea' player. I have invested in the best clubs, outfits and gadgets. Needless to say, it doesn't improve my game.

Bella

I manage to rearrange my Friday and Saturday clients. First thing Friday morning, the Bentley is loaded, and we are on the road up north.

I'm feeling really excited as well as a little nervous. I'm 99.9% sure my parents will be over the moon with the engagement and the baby. After all Damien did ask my dad before he proposed, so he knew it was coming. The baby is an added bonus. I just can't help but worry.

As we pull off the motorway I'm flooded with feelings and memories. Mostly good. But then my mind flicks to John. I still feel guilty about his death, even though he brought it on himself and almost killed me in the process. Damien takes my hand and gives it a little squeeze. He knows me so well.

"Mum, Dad. Damien and I have some news." I announce once we have been welcomed and consumed a copious amount of tea and biscuits. I have actually caught my dad looking at my engagement ring. My mum however is oblivious, caught up in the excitement of us being here. I'm not sure if my mum knows Damien had asked my dad for his blessing. I still can't get over the fact that big, powerful Damien King asked permission to do something from my Dad.

"You have?" My mum puts down her cup of tea. "Please tell me it's good news." She looks a little worried.

"Well, Damien and I are engaged."

"Oooooohh that's absolutely wonderful!" My mum jumps up and practically dives on Damien and me.

"Careful now." Says Damien to my mum.

"Careful? Why are you pregnant as well?" Mum jokes.

"Well actually…."

"Oh my goodness, Bella. My little girl." Mum is now in full blown tears.

"We are going to be grandparents Henry!" Dads stands and shakes Damien's hand while smacking him on the back as men do. Mum is hugging me, then kissing and stroking my face, then back to hugging. She is so excited. I too am filled with emotion. This moment I have dreamed of since I was little, and to make my parents this happy is extremely special.

We spend the day in the garden, catching up on each other news. I haven't told my parents about Chloe I have just said she's gone away on holiday with Josh. They would worry too much. It's been a lovely day and just what I needed. My parents garden is beautiful. It's full of colourful flowers and is always immaculate. There's are so many colourful butterflies, and birds which are so tame will take food out of your hand. It really is a lovely place to live.

I loved growing up here. It makes me think about our child. I hope I can give them a lovely childhood filled with happy memories. Maybe we should move back up here nearer to my parents, I would really like my mum near when I have the baby. It's funny how your dreams and focus's change. A couple of years ago my dream was to live in the city and live a busy lifestyle, but now, I'm wondering where would be the safest and most peaceful place to bring up my child. I wonder what Damien would think. I'll bring up the subject one day soon.

"Good night, Olivia, Henry." Damien says as he stands and holds out his hand to me. It's getting late and I have been yawning nonstop for the past hour. Damien has noticed but he has been having his ear chewed off by my dad. It's been hilarious to watch Damien's facial expressions. He's been waiting for that break in the conversation to escape.

"Good night you two, well three." Giggles my mum. I love seeing them so happy.

Damien and I are staying in the guest bedroom which used to be my room when I lived here. It's very surreal having this large alpha of a man in my bedroom. He looks even more huge than he normally does. I love that Damien respects my parents and stays here. He could insist we stay in a fancy hotel, but he doesn't, nor does he complain about the size of the bed, which is significantly smaller than the one we have a home. We snuggle up, and I fall asleep with the biggest smile on my face.

Saturday.

We have a lazy morning with my parents. My mum cooks us a full English breakfast and enjoys feeding Damien. Damien eats a lot especially when it comes to home-cooked food. I help mum with the dishes, and we potter about the house, while Damien and my dad read the papers and put the world to rights. I love how well he has settled into my family.

Damien has planned our day today. He has also firmly stated that the day has been paid for by him and he will under no circumstances accept any money from my father. It is his treat (well ours he actually said, but it's his money) and any offer will be seen as an insult. So, there you go Dad, no arguments.

The car picks us up at 1:00pm. It's not George our driver but Damien does seem to know him. Damien pops a bottle of champagne and pours it, handing my parents a glass. My mum is extremely impressed.

The car pulls up right outside the doors of the palace theatre. I had an idea this might be where we were going. Last night my mum mentioned that she hadn't been to the theatre for years and that she loved to go as a child with her mum, my grandma. I saw Damien's mind working as she told him.

"Oh my goodness! Damien, this is wonderful." My mum sobs happy tears as we all climb out of the car. We walk straight in and are greeted by the doorman by name. My Dad raises his eyebrows and I laugh. Yes dad, this is what life with Damien King is like, you better get used to it.

We are shown to our box and a gentleman takes our drinks and snacks order. I need all the snacks, this baby is hungry today. We have a perfect view of the stage from our box. I'm sat next to mum and she keeps squeezing my hand in excitement while point things out to me. She is in her element. Damien smiles as he watches her enjoy herself. Our child is so lucky to have Damien as their father. People in the audience look up to our box, obvious checking to see if we are celebrities. Dad pretends not to notice the attention, but I can see the pride in his eyes and body language.

The show is phenomenal. I'm an emotional wreck,

blooming hormones.

"Brilliant, absolutely brilliant. Not usually my kind of thing, the theatre, but I enjoyed that." My dad says as we make our way out of the box. The car is waiting for us outside the exit. It takes us to the restaurant Damien has made reservations at. My dad loves his steaks, so Damien has booked Hawksmoor, the best steaks in Manchester. The restaurant is located in a late Victorian courthouse. The interior is true to the building's features with a beautiful parquet floor, wood panelling, and clean brick walls. It's a lovely atmosphere.

Mum and dad get the Chateaubriand, Damien gets the Porterhouse and I get a Fillet. We all thoroughly enjoy our food while chatting and laughing the evening away. Mum and dad are telling Damien all sorts of stories of me growing up, they find them hilarious. I'm just sitting here storing the evening away in my memories. It's so lovely having my parents and Damien getting along so well.

Once our bellies are full, and I'm feeling a little tired, we head home.

Dad offers Damien a nightcap, but he refuses. He has not had a drop of alcohol since I told him I was pregnant. It's like he is pregnant too.

Sunday, Damien is up early getting ready for golf with my Dad. He is wandering around my bedroom in his expensive and very well-fitted golf attire. He is so goddam sexy. Even more so knowing he is doing this for my dad and me. Damien has been having lessons and learning all he can so him and my dad can have a good game. His bum in those silky trousers, yum. Damien catches me staring. His gazes turns dark. "You like what you see?"

"MMMmm I do." Damien looks at his watch.

"On your knees then my Bella, I've got 10 minutes."

The boys go off to golf in Damien's Bentley. My dad will be the talk of the golf club arriving in that. He looked very impressed when he got in it with his golf clubs.

Mum and I are going out wedding and baby shopping. Damien has arranged for the driver we had yesterday to take us around. Mum said she didn't mind driving, but Damien insisted as Damien does, and he is right, it will save us time having to find parking spaces everywhere.

First, we go to some bridal shops. Just to have a look. We haven't set a date or anything yet, although I know Damien would prefer sooner rather than later. I think we should wait until the baby is here. I would like to decide on my colour theme though at least. Plus, mum needs to know so she can get her outfit sorted, as that will take months knowing her.

We are having a lovely day, browsing. Mum's a little tipsy as we keep getting offered champagne, I'm just sticking to orange juice. That's another reason why I would like to get married after the baby has arrived, I want to be able to at least enjoy one glass of champagne on my wedding day. After our fill of weddings and before I need to carry my mum home, we go to some baby boutiques. We literally buy everything from dummies to prams.

"Are you sure Damien won't be upset that it's me here choosing your prams with you?"

"Of course not, and if he doesn't like the prams, I'm sure he can afford to buy another."

Yes, I have ordered 'Prams' plural. Well, if you can't have two when your fiancé is a billionaire then what is life all about? When I was little, I had a Silver Cross Balmoral dolls pram in red and white. I absolutely adored it. My mum has kept it in case she has any grandchildren. Anyway, the first shop we went in, there it was in full life size form. Mum and I gasped when we saw it.

"It's meant to be Bella." Said mum through her tears. So of course, that was pram number 1. Then I would need a pram that is more versatile, one that can be thrown in the boot and is easy to put up and down, so we got a silver cross travel system as well. After all the morning's excitement, we are both feeling "rather peckish", so we find a nice little café and order some lunch.

We are seated in a window seat watching the world go by and excitedly talking about our purchases, when a man walks past the window and stops in front of us. I recognise him, but I'm not sure where from. He looks at me with so much anger, my heart begins to beat faster and panic sets in. The man enters the café and storms over to our table.

Chapter 14

Bella

"How dare you show your face around here!"

"Don't you speak to my daughter like that!" but the guy continues as if mum hadn't said a word.

"You killed my best friend!" I now remember where I know him from. It's Shane, he was John's best friend, 'was' being to operative word. I haven't seen him for years. Neither had John. He hasn't aged well at all. He has long greasy hair swept up in a ponytail and a long unkept beard. He looks grubby and smells of chip fat.

"He killed himself! And rightly so after what he had done. He killed his own parents and would have killed Bella if it wasn't for Damien." My mum shouts, standing and confronting him. He kicks a chair in anger so I instinctively duck wrapping my arms around my stomach, protecting my baby. I hear the café door swing open with a bang, I look up to see Shane being pulled out of the café quicker than his feet can carry him. He's dragged around the side of the building. A minute later he appears scrabbling to his feet and running away, with what looks like two black eyes and a burst lip. Our driver then appears and comes into the café.

"Are you ok Bella? Did he hurt you?"

"No, I'm fine thank you. Just a bit shook up that's all."

"Damien is on his way." Of course he his. And of course, our driver for the day isn't just a driver. He is our bodyguard.

The waitress comes over to check we are alright and mum orders us some pots of tea.

"A cup of tea with 2 sugars will calm your nerves." she says to us both. Mum has insisted our driver sits down with us too. Mum is very grateful to our driver whose name is Frank. Mum thinks he is still just a driver who saw the commotion and came to our rescue. There's no point correcting her, it would make her worry.

Damien arrives shortly after.

"Bella are you ok? I think we should go to the hospital to get you and the baby checked out."

"Damien, I am fine and so is the baby." He worries so much. "It was an old friend of Johns, he is obviously still upset about losing him and needs someone to blame."

Damien nods and goes outside with Frank leaving dad with us.

"Well, I am glad you two ladies are ok. It was all very rushed. One minute we were in the clubhouse having a pint, the next Damien's phone pings and we are in his car doing hundreds of miles per hour, that car can really move."

"Yes, I think we have all had enough excitement for one day. Let's get Bella home." Mum ushers us both to get up.

When we get back to mum and dads I go for a bath. I think about what Shane said. When Damien rescued me, he told the police that John had heard him enter the house, so knowing his time was up John had killed himself. I have never asked Damien if that is what really happened. I am not sure if I want to know. I hate that John can still upset me. I need to not let him anymore. They say babies can feel what their mother feels. I'm not sure I believe it, but even so. I will not let John or anyone else upset my baby. We have had lovely day and I will not let anything spoil it.

I get dried and go downstairs. When I enter the lounge the talking stops and they all look at me with sympathetic faces. I don't like it.

"So did mum show you what we got today?" I say brightly

"No, I was waiting for you." Mum smiles.

"Ok well let's get it all out and have another look." I go to the hallway where all our shopping bags are, Damien helps me bring them into the lounge.

"Blooming heck, did you buy the whole shop?" Dad laughs

"This isn't all of it Henry, a lot of things we had to order, they will be delivered to Bella and Damien's house."

That night we have a Chinese takeaway and watch a film on dads dodgy TV box. It's another evening of love, laughter, and more memories made. The day's excitement with Shane was long forgotten.

Damien

It's Monday and we are driving home back to London. It's been a good weekend apart from the incident yesterday. Thankfully I had Frank there keeping an eye on them. It doesn't seem to have phased Bella though, she is happily flicking through the baby and wedding brochures she picked up with her mum.

"Have you thought about a date or a season you would like to get married in Damien?"

"Yes. What date is it today?"

"Umm, It's the 25th."

"Then the 25th."

"So the 25th, a year today, yes I am happy with that."

"No."

"No?"

"Not the 25th next year. The 25th today."

"Don't be silly. We can't get married today."

"We can. But that's up to you Bella." I don't think for one second Bella will agree to a wedding consisting of just us. I know she has dreamed of a big wedding since she was a little girl, and I would never take that away from her.

"I want you to be my wife. I don't care about a fancy wedding. All I want is you and me vowing to spend the rest of our lives together, being united in holy matrimony." Bella's eyes are beginning to fill up, I don't want to upset her.

"I understand you would like a spectacular wedding with all our friends and family, which is what you deserve and more. I will ensure you get it Bella. But I cannot wait for the day I can call you my wife. The day can't come soon enough. I want to be your next of kin. I want to be 'husband' on your pregnancy notes. I want you to be 'Mrs King' not 'Miss White' when we are called from the waiting room for our child's antenatal appointments. I am eternally grateful for you my Bella, so whatever you wish, I will make it be."

Bella lets out a sob and takes a deep breath. I am not sure if I have upset her or if it is her hormones. I don't think it's a good idea to ask, so I give her a minute to compose herself.

"Ok." She says, as she wipes her eyes in the passenger mirror.

"Ok what?"

"Ok, lets get married today." Surely she's not serious.

"But that's not what you want Bella?"

"I want a husband, a marriage, and to be married to the father of my child. The rest is only for a day. You are for the rest of my life." I cannot believe what I am hearing. I hope I can deliver on my promise of a marriage today. Before Bella can change her mind, I am on the phone to one of my connections who owes me a favour.

"Thank you and remember completely confidential."

"Of course Mr King."

"Oh my goodness Damien are well really doing this?" Bella beams with excitement.

"On one condition. We renew our vows once the baby is born with all our friends and family, and you have everything you ever dreamed of and more. No Expense spared for my wife. Promise me? I want you to have swans and doves, and whatever else people have at fancy weddings.

"Yes, then we can have Chloe and Josh by our side, and Dad can walk me down the aisle with my mum crying in the congregation." My parents would have loved Bella, and to see me get married. I'm sure they can see how happy I am, wherever they are. As my emotion rises, I quickly shut down those thoughts.

"Right, where shall we go for your dress? My beautiful wife needs a beautiful dress on her wedding day." Bella shrieks with excitement.

We go to Harrods and Bella chooses a stunning white and gold dress. With shoes, jewellery and hair clips to match, she couldn't look more beautiful.

"It's perfect Damien, Thank you." She beams while twirling around in the changing room mirror. I get suited up next. I normally have my suits tailored, but needs must, and the salesman knew what he was doing.

"It fits you perfectly."

"It's not bad. Now what colour tie?"

"How about gold to match my dress? Yes, this one

is perfect." Bella holds a tie up to my chest.

"Then this one it is."

The venue of our wedding is Mayfair library. Considering we have arranged this today, the venue couldn't be more perfect.

"Wow Damien, the library, is this where we are getting married?"

"It sure is." Bella loves to read, loves books and libraries. I couldn't have planned it any better.

The room is filled with flowers. Even I am impressed. There are all types and colours of blooms. With the wedding so last minute we cleared out two florists. But it was worth it. The look on Bella's face is priceless.

"Damien how did you do this? It's like something out of a fairy tale." I take Bella in my arms and kiss her. I then leave her at the end of the aisle and walk to the front. One of the witness's hands Bella a bouquet of white gerbera daisies. I specifically asked for those as when I proposed we were in a field full of daisies. There's a couple in the corner of the room who start playing 'Love Story' by Taylor Swift on the cello and violin.

Bella's eyes are full of emotion and as she begins to walk down the aisle, my breath catches. I try and make mental notes of everything. The way Bella looks, the way the room smells, full of the perfume of flowers, the sound of the music, and the way that I feel. It's incredible.

When its time for our vows, I speak from my heart.

"From the first moment I saw you, I knew you were meant for me.
The more time I spent with you, I knew I could never again let you be.
My love for you is infinite, I will cherish you for the rest of my life.
Please do me the honour, of becoming my wife?"

"I do." Bella sobs and I take her body in my arms, pressing her lips into mine.
I am the happiest man alive.

We sign the register and have a few photos taken.
"Where to now Wife?" I say as I open the door to the Bentley.
"Take me home, Husband." So I do.

It's Tuesday, my happy bubble, is well and truly burst. I'm out with a client when Mike calls.
"Boss, another delivery arrived for Bella today. A pig's head with its eyes removed." How is this guy outsmarting us.
"It is a completely different person doing the delivery every time. The order is always made with a different mobile number that is not linked to anyone. The only thing we know is when the orders are made, the phones are always in London,

within about a 5 miles radius."

"And Bella is unaware?"

"Yes. The delivery was intercepted at the hotel door."

"Keep me posted."

Once I have finished with my client I go to salon and work from my office there. I want to check on my wife. I hear her before I see her, chatting away to one of her clients.

"Speak of the devil." She says as I walk over and give her a kiss on the cheek.

"I thought my ears were burning."

Bella introduces me to her client, an older lady who seems to care for Bella a lot. Once Bella has finished her clients for the day, we leave everyone to close up and I take Bella home.

"I have enrolled for the pregnancy yoga, I start on Thursday."

I was hoping to go along with her, but I have a meeting I can't get out of on Thursday.

"That's wonderful, Frank will drive you."

"I'm sure I won't need protection from a bunch of down-dogging pregnant ladies." Bella laughs. Thankfully Bella isn't aware of the threatening deliveries, and that's how I intend it to stay.

"Well, just for my peace of mind. At least for the first couple of weeks."

"Ok" Bella says as she rolls her eyes.

Bella

Thursday soon came around.

"Today we have a new member, her name is Bella."
"Hi Bella." The group says simultaneously. I take a seat on one of the free mats.

We start by doing a warm-up, our first yoga pose is something called the cat-cow stretch. Which apparently is "a gentle way to wake up your spine and helps get the baby in the best position." I used to do yoga years ago, so I am familiar with a lot of the poses and stretches, but there are a few that I haven't heard of before. The animal names still make me giggle.

After the class everyone goes into the café for a drink. The instructor asks me to join them. I suddenly get a wave of anxiety. I panic about what I would say and how I would come across, I wasn't prepared for this. I thank her and make an excuse about needing to be somewhere. This is when I need Chloe, she would tell me to "Put your big girl pants on and show them how wonderful you are." But she's not here, so I don't. Maybe I will next week, I will prepare myself for it. If I know something is going to happen, I can get my head around it beforehand. I will think of things I might say to people, questions I might ask them, and answers to questions they may ask me. When a situation like that is sprung on me, I panic. Frank is waiting for me by the door, he hears my little white lie but doesn't falter.

"Where to now Mrs King?" Wow, I don't think I will ever get tired of hearing that. That's something else I will have to explain, and I need to get my story straight. Everyone is sure to wonder who Frank is. What do I say "oh he's just my bodyguard." I could get away with saying he's just my driver, but I need him to wait in the car, not stand at the door staring everyone out. I will speak to Damien. The yoga class is in a church hall. There's only one way in and one way out. Frank can park right outside the doors, surely Damien will agree to that.

"Straight home please Frank." I have some salon admin I want to catch up on, I also want to go online and order myself a few new gym yoga outfits. Mine were feeling a little tight today so I need to get some maternity ones, plus most of the girls were wearing short tops showing off their bumps, I want to do that too. My phone rings, It's Damien.

"Hello Mrs King." He says in his deep, gruff, sexy voice.

"Mmm I love it when you call me that. But don't let anyone hear yet."

"Of course. Close staff are aware and are under strict instructions to only call you Mrs King when you are alone or with myself. How was yoga?"

"It was good, I really enjoyed it, I feel so energised now, I feel like I could run a marathon."

"No marathon running please. Good I am glad you enjoyed it."

"I was thinking next time, Frank could wait in the car. I'd really like to stay and have a coffee with everyone after the class, but I know people will be asking who Frank is. I would rather just say he is my driver. Plus, there really isn't any need for him to be there. It's just a group of ladies doing some stretches."

"I will speak to Frank. Where are you heading now?"

"Just home, I have some admin from the salon to do and I want to do some online shopping."

"Ok, don't work too hard, make sure you rest. I will be home for dinner."

"Great, I will cook."

"Wonderful, until then my Bella." The way he says "My Bella" still does all sorts of crazy things to my body.

I set up my laptop on the kitchen island. I put on some music and enjoy the afternoon working and pottering about in the kitchen. Other than not being able to see or speak to Chloe I am feeling really good. I have a wonderful husband, a baby on the way, and a beautiful home, I couldn't be happier.

That is until the next day when things start to go south.

Chapter 15

Bella

It's a busy day in the salon, even with my reduced clients and larger appointment times I am still rushing about. It's an entertaining day though. I have a real giggle with one of my older ladies. The lady is in her 80s and comes in every week for a shampoo and set. She has been having a set for many years and they're not the most comfortable of services, your hair wound tightly around plastic spikey rollers. There are lots of other ways of achieving a similar style now and I wonder if she would like to try something different for a change. She is a little hard of hearing, so I ask her again louder and using less words.

"Do you like having sets?"

"Oh, I used to."

"So, you don't anymore?"

"No, my husband passed away about 10 years ago, I haven't had any since."

I look at her in confusion until the penny drops. Oh gosh did she really think I just asked her if she likes having sex? I see my face redden in the mirror.

My embarrassment soon turns to laugher when I explain to the lady what I actually said.

There's never a dull day when you're a hairdresser.

My last client of the day cancels, so I decide to go down and see Tiffany on the front desk.

"Bella! I'm so glad you're here. I am soooo bored. Tell me about your day."

While I am filling Tiffany in on my day, I hear raised voices at the front door. The security guards are stopping a man carrying a package entering the hotel. I hear him say my name. I excuse myself from Tiffany and get closer.

"I have strict instructions to give this parcel to Bella White."

"And we have strict instructions not to let you in!"

"Excuse me I am Bella White, I can take that?"

"No Miss, we cannot let you take this parcel."

"Why not? It is addressed to me."

"We have been told under no circumstances does any parcel addressed to you enter this hotel without it being checked first."

"Is that so, and who told you this?" I say with my hands on my hips, as if I need to ask.

"ME!" growls Damien from behind me. I turn to see my husband looking furiously at the security guards. They obviously said too much. Sheepishly they return to their post and escort the delivery guy out of sight of the hotel.

"Damien? What is going on? Why are all my deliveries to be checked before I receive them?"

"It's just a precaution, all staff are to have their delivery's and post checked, its policy for everyone."

"Well, it didn't sound that way to me, it sounded as if this treatment was just for me. So can I have my parcel then?"

"No. Were you not listening to me? It needs to be checked first." Damien snatches the parcel from the security guard and storms off into the hotel. I'm fuming. How dare he speak to me like that. I run back to Tiffany who has been watching the whole incident from her desk.

"Hey don't get upset. You'll upset the baby. He's probably just having a bad day." There's something he's not telling me, I am sure of it.

"Hey how about you, me and Katie go out for drinks, well food for you, drinks for us? How about it? A girl's night. I finish in half an hour."

"Great yes, I'll ring Katie, she should be finished with her last client now."

Damien

Furious is an understatement. I cannot believe the imbeciles on the hotel doors. Why did they think it was appropriate to tell my Bella her parcels needed to be checked? Have they too few brain cells to make something up, or to say nothing at all?! I slam my office door shut and rip open the parcel. Inside there is a vacuumed packed clear plastic bag containing what looks like some form of animal guts. It's full of blood, it's revolting. I throw it back in the box and call Mike to come in.

I ask Mike to get rid of it and think of an alternative

gift we can get to give Bella in replacement. I get on the phone and give my team a kick up the arse. Jobs and restrictions are not to be discussed with anyone other than King staff and this moron who has a death wish sending my Bella crazy sh*t had better be caught ASAP. I pay them enough.

Once I have calmed down, I ring Bella. She doesn't answer. I ring her again, still doesn't answer. I ring Frank, and he answers on the first ring.
"Are you with Bella?"
"I am. Bella, Tiffany, and Katie are having dinner at Lucia, the Italian restaurant on the next road down. I drove them here and I am sat meters away at the bar, I have my eyes on them and the doors."
"Good. Stay put I will be along shortly." Bella's obviously annoyed with me. I was a little harsh when I spoke to her. I will apologise. I am starting to lose my head again. I detest not being in control of a situation.
I arrive at the restaurant and join Frank at the bar. Bella looks like she is having a good time. Her and Katie are laughing at something Tiffany is saying. It is nice to see her so relaxed.
I have spoken to Josh today. He and Chloe have settled in well. Chloe seems to be keeping him on his toes. Thankfully we have made some progress on Chloe's case. We have a name for the gunman. His name is Cain Graves, none other than the estranged son of Mr Graves. The very Mr Graves whom we have been working with. This was my

meeting today. Mr Graves had requested an urgent meeting with me. Cain Graves originally worked for his father until he went rogue. Cain hadn't had the same values as his father. Don't get me wrong, Mr Graves is no saint, but if someone had paid their debt, their business with them would be done. Cain would kill the person anyway. This is where Graves 'Company' began to get an extremely bad reputation. It then resulted in gag wars. Graves lost many friends and family members due to this, hence why he asked for our company's help. It is only a matter of time now until we track him down. Graves explained Cain is extremely good at keeping under the radar. Cain has exceptional skills in IT and is very intelligent. He does however have a bad temper which leads him to make mistakes. Hopefully, he will make one soon, and when he does, we will be waiting.

Three men make their way over to the girl's table. I stiffen in my seat. I see Frack in the corner of my eye turn to look at me. He is obviously waiting for my reaction. I try and keep calm as there's nothing wrong with a friendly bit of chit chat. The other girls are single, and I do not want to upset Bella anymore today by making her uncomfortable. I will just sit here with my drink and observe. I watch them like a hawk. One of them in particular cannot take his eyes of my Bella. My hands tighten into fist. There's a chuckle sound from the side of me. I turn to see Frank hiding a smirk behind his glass of coke.

"Something funny Frank?!"

"No Boss." He straightens in his chair and his serious face returns.

One of the men has the girls in hysterics. I don't like them. They all look like they're on a set of The Only Way is Essex. With their fake tan and turkey teeth. One of them is actually pouting. The three of them disperse around the table. Each one stands beside one of the girls, hooking an arm around the back of their chair. The guy next to Bella bends to say something in her ear. His hand brushes her bare shoulder as he does. That's it. I have seen enough. I am stood beside them in a heartbeat.

"What's up Mate?" why do imbeciles insist on calling people they just meet 'Mate' I am far from your mate, boy.

I stare at him for a second before I speak. My voice comes out in a deep growl as I try to control my anger.

"Nobody touches what is mine."

"Damien?" Bella breathes quietly asking me to calm down. But I cannot. I see red. I see how he is looking at my Bella and I lose it.

"Remove your hand from her chair. If you touch her again, I will crush your fingers so intensely you will never be able to touch anything ever again!" the guy is looking at me with furrowed brows deciding his next move.

"Let's go Damien." Bella says as she stands and gathers her purse and phone. I am frozen to the spot for a minute staring down the boy who thinks he can touch my wife and get away with it. Frank taps me on the shoulder pulling me out of my trance. I follow him and Bella out of the restaurant, we get into the car in silence.

Nobody says a word on the way back to Kingston Manor. I start to calm down and feel ashamed of my actions today. What must Bella think of me? I despise the fact I have upset her. She would understand if I could tell her the truth. That there is some psychopath out there sending her horrifying packages and that the said psycho could very well have been that guy. Maybe I should tell her the truth. No, then her anxiety would escalate and could affect the baby. Although at least then I could keep her at home, safe.

These packets aren't just to scare Bella, they are a warning, a sign of what is to come. And I will be ready.

I'll never lose her again.

Bella

My heart is breaking a little. I am so confused as to why Damien is acting like this. Is the pressure of becoming a father getting to him? Have I done something wrong to make him not trust me? Damien follows me into the kitchen. I get a bottle of water out of the fridge and when I turn, he is stood behind me.

"Look at me Bella." I do.

"Forgive me for losing my temper. I am stressed and when I saw you being touched by another, I lost my head."

"He was hardly touching me Damien. His hand brushed my shoulder. I told him I wasn't interested. Why can you not trust me?"

"I do trust you, its everyone else I do not trust." Damien wraps his arms around me and kisses my head. "I'm sorry, I love you so much." I am too tired to continue speaking about it.

"I love you too. I'm tired. I'm going to bed."

I get into bed and lie worrying about Damien. We need to make an appointment soon with our counsellor Dr. McGrain. Damien has always had a temper, but never towards me. He still blames himself for what happened to me, he is so scared of anything happening again, he gets extremely over protective. But that's all in the past. He needs to realise I am safe now. Me and the baby are going to be fine.

I make a mental note to book an appointment in the morning and I fall asleep.

The week passes quickly. It is really busy at work and when I'm not at the salon, I am sleeping. Thursday cannot come soon enough, my day off. A lie in and pregnancy yoga class is just what I need.

My new yoga outfit has arrived, I have mentally prepared for conversations after the class. Damien has agreed that Frank will wait in the car, on one condition, additional security was to be put up in the church hall. Damien has done this at his own expense of course. The hall now has a high tech security camera and entrance system where a security code or card is needed to enter the building. A little over the top in my opinion. Anyhow, he's happy and so am I.

I find myself a mat and wait for the class to start. A few of the girls make light conversation with me and I feel a lot more relaxed.

"Girls, today we have another new member, please welcome Anna." Anna is looking around trying to find somewhere to sit, there's a spare mat next to me so I give her a wave and point beside me. She smiles gratefully and comes over.

"Thank you for that."

"My pleasure. I was new last week so I know how you feel. I'm Bella by the way."

"Nice to meet you Bella, I'm Anna."

I really enjoy the class again, we do some new poses and stretches, one in particular gives me the giggles 'The Angry Cat' this position is supposed to help with back pain. It also seems to release wind for some ladies too. Unfortunately for Anna, the lady in front of her did just that.

After the class we all go into the café and get a coffee. Anna comes too and sits next to me.

"I really enjoyed that, I think I will come again next week."

"Yes, me too. I always feel really good afterwards. It's just what I needed after the week I have had."

Anna smiles and nods.

"I understand."

We sit for about an hour getting to know each other. Anna just moved here with her husband, but he works away a lot, so she has a lot of time on her own.

"We can meet up outside of yoga if you like, I can show you around?"

"That would be brilliant thank you." We swap numbers and arrange to meet on Monday.

It's another crazy weekend at the salon and Damien seems extremely distracted.

Chapter 16

Bella

"I want to speak to your manager." Spits the extremely hairy woman in front of me.

"I am the manager, and I am asking you and your family to leave." Mike appears behind me.

"You heard the boss, out!" The woman, her daughters and goodness knows who else the other three family members were she brought to one of her daughters haircut appointments, finally leave the salon.

"Right guys, I need this whole area sterilising along with the equipment and trolley, the gown needs going on a boiled wash. In fact, just bag it and bin it." Seriously, I will never understand some people. My last client was a teenage girl. She came into the salon with a full family entourage.

The appointment was for a cut and blow dry. I seated her at my station and started to carry out my consultation. When sectioning the girl's black hair, the underneath looked grey. Confused I looked closer and to my horror realised that the hair was so covered with head lice and eggs it had made her hair look grey.

I was very polite at first but there's no getting

through to some people, it went something like this:

"I'm so sorry, I will be unable to do your daughters hair today, she has headlice." I say to the mother as quietly and respectfully as I can. The woman looks at me in confusion. I can tell her first language isn't English, so at first, I am not sure she has understood, but she eventually speaks.

"I know this. This why we come for haircut. To get rid of insect."

"I can't carry out any services on her hair for risk of cross infection unfortunately. There's a chemist just down the road, they will recommend suitable products. If you get her treated, I will gladly book her back in and restyle her hair."

"No, you cut her hair now. We no leaving until she had haircut."

And you know the rest. I feel extremely sorry for the girl. She must have had those lice for a long time. It must be extremely uncomfortable. It's child neglect really.

Saturday evening Damien takes me out for dinner. Frank takes us again and I'm starting to wonder why. Frank is not just a driver, he is a trained bodyguard, unlike our usual driver George. Damien must still be fearing for my safety. It will probably be because of the situation with Chloe. The sooner they find him the better for all of us. Frank takes us out of town to a little family-owned Italian restaurant. Italian is my favourite.

Damien opens the door for me and pulls out my chair for me to sit down. Always the perfect gentleman. The restaurant is typical old Italian, with its red, green and white tablecloth and napkins. The candles are in the top of old wine bottles and there are different colours of hard wax dripping down the sides. It's a lovely cosy atmosphere. We are seated at a table for two. Damien's big knees touch mine under the table. He takes my hand in his and looks at me with those big, deep, dark eyes. Tingles spread throughout my body making me warm inside.

"I love you Bella King."

"Love you too Damien King." I know he can be a grump and lose his temper, but he would never hurt me or our baby. I trust him with all my heart and if he thinks we need protecting for whatever reason, I won't fight him on that.

Monday comes around and I am out shopping with my new friend Anna. Anna is really lovely. She tells me all about her husband and he's very much like Damien. He has a demanding powerful job and a short fuse but is always exceptionally kind to her. This is their first baby too and she is the same weeks pregnant as me give or take a few days. It's like she was sent from Chloe to look after me until she returns. I have been feeling so lost without her. Katie and Tiffany are great, but I don't feel I can share any personal details about my relationship with Damien with them, as technically I am Katie's boss and Damien is Tiffany's.

We meet at Starbuck's and get Caramel Frappuccino's, which seem to be becoming a craving of mine. Then we go to Mamas and Papas and coo over all the baby stuff. It's so nice having someone to do this with. We stop for lunch, and I notice Frank lurking about outside.

"So, what's the deal with your driver then? He hardly takes his eyes off you. It seems wherever you are, there he is a few feet behind?"

"He's kind of a bodyguard as well as a driver."

"A bodyguard? What do you need a bodyguard for?"

"Nothing really, Damien is just really overprotective."

"A bit over the top I'd say." I don't expect Anna to understand, and I won't be explaining myself to her in any more detail. I don't want to go through the whole 'John' scenario. I change the subject back to babies and we continue with our lunch.

"Let's have dessert?"

"No honestly, I'm full up." And I'm actually feeling a bit sick.

"I think I'm going to go home if that's ok Anna?"

"Sure, I'll see you on Thursday at yoga?"

"Definitely, see you then."

Frank takes me home and I go straight to bed. I feel sick and dizzy. I thought my morning sickness was starting to go but obviously not. I fall asleep as soon as my head hits the pillow. Damien is there when I wake up. Sat on the bed at the side of me watching me sleep.

"How are you feeling now? Do I need to call the doctor?"

I sit up in bed, I feel like the room is spinning.

"I still feel a little off." I lie. "But a lot better than I did. I am still rather tired though, so I am going to stay in bed is that ok?"

Damien leans in and kisses my head.

"Of course, whatever you need. Can I get you anything?"

"I'm fine, I just need sleep."

I lie back down and close my eyes. The room is spinning. I feel like I've had a night on the town and drank too many vodkas. Pregnancy is crazy.

The rest of the week I feel fine. On Thursday after yoga we all meet in the café and have lunch. I am really enjoying being with other expecting mums. I know Damien is pleased I have made some new friends. He worries too much about me. We are all having such a good time sharing our pregnancy stories. We take a few selfies as girls do and I send one to Damien so he can see I am ok and enjoying myself.

Damien

Bella's at pregnancy yoga today but I decide to work from my office at the salon as its near to the church hall where the class is. We are making good progress with Cain. We have found his hide out and only missed him by a couple of hours. The end is near.

I'm busy on the phone when Mike comes in without knocking. I know this means there's an issue that can't wait. I end the call and look at Mike. He is holding another package.

"Another one?"

"Yes boss, but this one is addressed to you." Mike hands me the parcel. It is the same packaging and label as the ones Bella has been receiving but this one is indeed addressed to me. I open the package cautiously. Again, it's a plastic vacuum sealed, blood filled packet. But as I move it between my fingers, I see something inside. The instant I see what it is, I feel sick. It's an animal foetus. I pick up my phone and ring Frank.

"Do you have eyes on Bella."

"I have visual on the live security footage. She is sat with the girls from the yoga class having lunch. Everything seems ok boss."

While Frank speaks my phone pings, it's a message from Bella. A photo of all the girls together laughing and smiling...... I stare at the photo in disbelief. It can't be. There's no way.

"Frank, get Bella out of there right now! Tell her there's been a family emergency and get her in the car immediately. I'm on my way."

I run through the hotel and out onto the street. I see red and power through the streets with no concern for anyone else. I must get to Bella. I hope I am not too late. The church hall is only a few blocks away but it feels like an eternity trying to get to the end. I eventually see the car, Bella is in the window looking confused at the sight of me running full throttle in my 3 piece suit. Diving into the back seat. I pull Bella into my arms.

"Frank, get us to the hospital. Now!" Frank accelerates as he pulls out, pushing us back into our seats.

"Damien, what is going on? You are scaring me."

"How do you feel?"

"What? How do I feel? I feel confused and worried. Why are we going to the hospital?"

"Do you have any pain? Or sickness?"

"Well, I have just started to feel a little dizzy and sick again, like I did on Monday. But other than that, I'm fine, no pain, nothing. I really don't need to go to the hospital."

"On Monday what did you do?"

"I met Anna from yoga, I told you about her. We went shopping and then for lunch."

"That photo you sent me earlier. Show me Anna on there." I hold my phone out to Bella, she points to the woman sitting next to her.

"S**T!"

I punch the seat in between my legs.

"Damien what is it?" Bella cries. I need to get it together. I hear Josh in my head. "FOCUS!"

"Bella." I take her hand in mine, she's shaking. "I need you not to panic. Everything is going to be fine. I don't even know how this is possible, but I am almost certain that the girl you call Anna, is not Anna at all, she is…………. Claire.

Chapter 17

Damien

It takes Bella a few seconds to register who Claire is.

"Claire? As in Pete's sister Claire? The Claire who killed herself and everyone blamed you, Claire?" I nod. I can't believe the words I am saying, but I would recognise that face anywhere. That face has haunted my dreams for years.

"You're probably absolutely fine Bella, but we need to get your checked out. If she is back, we need to expect the worse just to be safe."

"I do feel sick and dizzy Damien. But what could she have done?"

I don't want to spell it out to Bella but the fact that she felt sick and dizzy on Monday when she was with Claire and feels the same today, terrifies me.

"Try not to worry. I have my medical team meeting us at the hospital. They will check everything and ensure you're perfectly healthy."

"What about the baby Damien?"

"The baby too, everything will be fine." I pull Bella into me and hold her tightly. I don't want anything to happen to our baby, but I cannot live without my Bella.

We are met at the hospital doors by my team with a wheelchair. I can see Bella wants to reject it, but she doesn't. We march down to the assessment room and immediately they get to work. Bella's complexion has already started to change. She is looking very pale.

"I'm fitting an ID and taking some blood. The results could take hours to come back, it would help if we knew what she has ingested. Time is of the essence I'm afraid." I nod to the doctor. We need to get Claire.

"I'll be right outside, I just need to make a phone call." I kiss Bella and call Mike.

"I've sent you the photo and Frank will send you the security footage. Find her immediately. This is potentially life or death where my wife and child are concerned."

"We will find them boss."

When I get back into the room Bella is being sick into a bowl.

"Most of her stomach is empty now. I am just concerned about what has already entered her bloodstream. Hopefully it is minimal."

"See everything is going to be alright, My Bella." Bella's smiles wearily. I'm not sure if she believes me or not. The fact that she is already showing symptoms isn't a good sign. Obviously a large enough amount has entered her blood to make her body react that way.

"I feel like I need to sleep." I look at the doctor and he nod's.

"You go ahead and get some rest. We will look after you."

I sit and hold Bella's hand while she sleeps, I pray to every god in the universe. Please let my Bella be ok, please let my baby be ok. I am lost in my own thoughts when my phone alerts me to a message.

Mike: We got her. On way to the office.

I kiss Bella on the forehead. "I love you my Bellas." I explain to the doctor and he assures me Bella will probably sleep for the next few hours. I will hopefully be back before she wakes. Anything I can find out about what Bella has ingested will help the doctors, so I must try.

Frank pulls up outside the office in record time. I sit for a minute before I exit. Anger has built inside me and I am not sure I can be in the same room as someone who has hurt my wife and child. Let alone Claire who is supposedly dead. I need to compose myself. I need to get all the information I can from her.

"Damien." Claire smiles when she greets me as if we a long-lost friends. She stands from her chair and is swiftly forced back down by my men who stand beside her. "It's so good to see you." She beams. The woman is a nutcase. I am unsure of how to pursue it. I would normally threaten and beat people I need information from. I decide to let her take the lead.

"I have been waiting so long for this day Damien.

Are you not going to speak? Come on, how surprised are you to see me?" she giggles, this woman is on drugs.

"Surprised does not cover what I feel right now Claire."

"I knew it, I knew you would be happy to see me."

Anger builds inside me.

"What the hell is this Claire! What the F**K have you given to my wife?!" so much for keeping my cool. I kick a chair and it flies across the room banging into a filing cabinet.

Claire jumps and her expression changes to confusion.

"Your wife? Don't be ridiculous, she's not your wife." Claire laughs nervously.

"What have you given her Claire?"

"You weren't supposed to marry her Damien! You were supposed to marry me!"

She's breaking now, starting to sweat and shake. Putting her head in her hands she screams.

"And You're supposed to be dead Claire!"

"It's all my stupid brother's fault. He couldn't finish the job, so I had to do it for him."

"Did Pete know you were still alive?"

"No. I just kept him riled up over the years. Making sure he was aware of your happy life, and success and how it wasn't fair on our family. Strategically placed photos and news articles. Post and deliveries, you can imagine, I'm sure. I can get quite creative when I put my mind to it." She winks at me which ignites the fire building inside me even more.

"I wanted you to feel the pain I had. Make you realise what you had lost. I enjoyed watching you suffer over the years. My plan all along was to come back to you. I just needed you to be ready, to have learnt your lesson. I have watched you throughout your adult life. Always alone, never had a relationship. I know it's because you missed and loved me too much. You couldn't be with anyone else. I was getting ready to return to you. I was coming back to you when you needed me the most when your father died. But then she turned up and brainwashed you. And now she's trapped you with a baby!" Claire stands as she shouts, evil spilling from her every pore. "You need to see what she is Damien! I have come back for you. I forgive you! We are meant to be together!"

"ENOUGH!" I storm over to her and put my face in hers. "What have you given her Claire?"

"I have simply taken care of our problem. You just need to get over the shock and then you will see everything has worked out perfectly."

"Get it into your head right now. I love my wife. I do not love you. We will never be together. I despise you!"

"It's not true!" Claire screams as she lunges towards me. I grab her by the throat and throw her up against the wall.

"Tell me what you gave her." I squeeze her neck and cut off her air supply. Panic fills her eyes. She realises I am not messing about. Her lips move as if she is trying to speak. I release my grip slightly so she can answer me.

"Ricin." She splutters.

I immediately throw her to the floor and call the hospital. The Doctor answers on first ring.

"Ricin?"

"I thought as much. There's no antidote as such unfortunately, but we've given her plenty of fluids which is the best thing, it will eventually flush out of her system. We got to her in time Mr King. But the next 48 hours will be crucial for your child."

I end the call and stare at the evil woman sat on the floor holding her neck.

"Does anyone else know you are still alive? Family? Friends?"

"No." she whispers still holding her throat. "I was going to surprise them... Say I'd lost my memory but now it had returned, or something like that." She coughs.

"Good, nobody will notice you have gone missing, and nobody can be charged for killing someone who is already dead." Claire looks at me with complete shock. Did she really think this would end how she wanted?

"Get rid of her!" I say to the guys as I walk out of the door. I need to get back to my wife.

The next 48 eight hours are long, mentally and emotionally draining. Bella is in and out of consciousness, but when she wakes, I'm positive and attentive. I fill her with as much hope and love as I can in those minutes, then when she sleeps, I break with worry and panic. I'm furious with myself for letting that woman get near my Bella. I know from experience that blaming myself does not help but I cannot understand why I didn't see this earlier. When Bella was receiving the parcels, I should have known that it was a woman's doing. But when you attend someone's funeral, see their coffin being laid into the ground, albeit from a distance, behind a tree, as I was not welcome, you do wholeheartedly believe they are dead. My mind is in overdrive. I haven't slept a wink.

After the 48 hours are up, we wait for the doctor arrive. I hold Bella's hand as we pray for good news on how Bella and our baby are. These next few moments will change our life one way or another. I'm sat on the bed beside Bella, she snuggles in to me further. Her breath hitches as she tries to hold back her tears. I put my arm around her and squeeze. Kissing the top of her head I say "Everything is fine. I love you."
The doctor walks through the door with charts in his hands.

Chapter 18

Bella

Please be ok, please be ok, I pray.

"Good news, all your bloods have come back normal, so that's no damage to any of your organs, your blood pressure and heartrate are now at normal levels so I am pleased with that.

"And my baby?"

"Your hormone levels are what we would expect at this many weeks which is a good sign. I'd like to do another scan so we can visibly check how they're doing." Damien squeezes my hand.

"See everything is going to be fine my Bellas." I love how he calls us 'Bellas' plural. I just hope it continues.

I'm put in a wheelchair and taken down to maternity. All I can do is pray in my head, 'Please be ok, Please .' Damien and the doctor make small talk on the way, but all I can focus on is my prayers of hope. We are taken into a private room. I get on the bed with Damien's help, he stands beside me holding my hand. The gel and the camera are placed on my tummy and the room goes silent as the sonographer looks at the screen.

It feels like hours of the camera moving over and

around pushing and prodding until finally she turns the screen around to face me and Damien.

"Everything looks fine." I take a deep breath and realise I have been holding my breath this whole time. The sound of a baby's heartbeat fills the room, I cry tears of happiness and relief. I look at Damien whose eyes are glazed. He smiles and nods. I know his silence is because if he says a word, he will break too. He kisses the top of my head and stays there stroking my hair while the sonographer finishes her checks.

"All the baby's organs look to be working fine, the heart rate is good. The placenta looks fine as well. I would like to monitor you closely for a while. A scan every week for the next few weeks. Obviously, everything looks fine now but we cannot be 100% sure if there has been any damage we are unable to see, and unfortunately we won't find that out until the baby is born. From what I can see today baby is happy and healthy."

So, we aren't out of the woods yet. But it is still good news. I suppose they could never say for certain. My maternal instinct to protect, just doubled somehow. I am not going to let anything else happen to my baby ever again.

Two weeks later I've given up work, I have not left the house apart from to go to my scan appointments. Everything is still looking good with baby King, but I won't stop worrying until I am holding our baby in my arms. I have spent my days eating everything it tells me to in my baby book, having a leisurely swim and reading. Damien has not left the house either. He has been working from home and checking on me every hour. I can tell he is getting frustrated being kept inside all day everyday.

"Right, we are going away for a few days, what shall I pack for you?" Damien says as he storms into our bedroom interrupting my reading and opening my wardrobes.

"I don't want to go anywhere, I'm fine here."

"No, you're not. You and the baby need some fresh air, a change of scenery. It's just a few days."

"I want to stay here Damien."

"My Bella." Damien sits on the bed beside me. "I know you are scared. But stressing and worrying isn't doing you or the baby any good. We need to take our minds off things. Focus on us."

"Where to?" I ask still not sure if I should go.

"A cottage near the sea. We need some sea air. I have it all arranged. It's safe and nobody knows us. There's a quiet village that we can go to if you desire, if not we shall stay by our log fire at night and walk along the seafront in the day."

It does sound pretty good. Even though Kingston has everything and more, sometimes it can feel a little suffocating, especially right now.

"Ok?" Damien smiles jumping up, he takes out my suitcase and starts putting random clothes in it.

"Arrhh forget it," he throws the case on the floor. "We will buy new when we get there, let's just go."

I laugh, which is probably the first time I have laughed in weeks.

"Don't be ridiculous Damien, let me do it. You go pack your things." I say, as I take the net dress out of my case which I wore for Halloween last year. Honestly.

As we pull off the motorway Damien puts the roof down on the Bentley. The smell of the sea air hits my lungs, relaxing me instantly. This was a good idea.

We arrive at the cottage on the seafront. It's a beautiful white stone with pastel green sash windows and door. There are window boxes full of colourful flowers, a little white fence with a gate surrounds an immaculate lawn. Damien opens my door and gives me his hand to help me out of the car. My gentleman. He leads us down the path to the front door, I can hear wind chimes playing cheerful tunes in the breeze, the crashing of the sea and laughing from the seagulls above us, perfect.

Damien puts a code in a very expensive and brand-new looking lock on the front door, I then notice all the security cameras. My stomach flips with the memory of why we need these. I need to ignore them and just enjoy where we are.

Inside the cottage it is light and airy. To the right there's the living room with two large sofas, a fluffy sheep skin rug on the wooden floor, and a large log burner with logs stacked up at the side. To the left is the kitchen, dining room. The Kitchen is a pastel green with thick wooden worktops. French doors lead out onto a lovely terrace and garden filled with all kinds of flowers and fruit trees.

"It's perfect Damien."

"And so are you." He kisses my cheek and then wanders around the kitchen opening and closing cupboard doors. He looks so sexy in his grey jogging bottoms and tight black T shirt. His hair is loose, not his usual styled to perfection and his face has natural stubble. I love him like this. Relaxed and just him.

"So what would you like to do first?" I ask, to which Damien turns to face me raising an eye brow.

"First, I would like to 'do' my wife." Mmm I love it when he calls me wife.

"Oh yeah and what is it you would like to 'do' to your wife?"

"Get up those stairs right now and I will show you!" he lunges towards me, I run up the stairs with him following right behind. He playfully smacks my bum as he catches up to me.

Damien

After getting a fill of my wife and making sure she feels completely loved and satisfied, we go for a walk in the village. It's a busy little place with mainly locals but a few tourists. The tourists stand out like sore thumbs, especially Bella and I.

Everyone is very friendly, stopping to say hello and make general small talk. Bella seems happier and relaxed which I am pleased about, I unfortunately cannot say the same about myself. Last night Penny answered a call from Chloe. Penny followed instructions, telling Chloe Bella wasn't there and had gone away. I didn't sleep all night. Something is about to happen I can feel it. I am ready for this to be the end of the nightmare. Still not fully aware of Cains where abouts I decided to get away from London. The main reason being that I need to be closer to Josh in case I am needed, and I have to keep Bella away from any trouble. There's only me from Kings security who knows where Josh and Chloe are. I can't risk Cain finding out. I'm hoping he shows up at Kingston where my men are ready and waiting but I think he is more intelligent than that.

"Can we go in here?" Bella tugs my arm towards a second-hand bookshop.

"Of course."

Bella browses happily like she hasn't a care in the world. There are old books and new. I watch as Bella's fingers tips slide gently over the spines of the books, until she sees something that catches her eye and removes it from the shelf. The excited expression on her face as she thinks of the story beneath those pages and the people that have gotten lost in them before her. This is what she deserves, this is what I will give her and my child everyday of their lives. Once Cain is out of the picture, I will ensure that. After picking out a few old romance books, Bella pays, and we continue our stroll down the cobbled street.

"What do you fancy for your dinner? I'll cook, anything you'd like?" I say as I point to a nice-looking butchers.

We choose some steaks for dinner, some bits for breakfast bacon, sausage, as well as a few other items the butcher recommended. We then go to the greengrocers next door and now have bags full of food which will last us days. Once we get back to the cottage, I light the log fire and start preparing dinner. Bella gets changed into her PJ's and sits on the sofa in front of the fire reading one of her new books.

After dinner I ring Josh again. Still no answer. I have been trying since we received the call from Chloe. We aren't scheduled to ring until tomorrow, so Josh doesn't have a reason to be near the phone. As it's a discreet radio phone, there is only a small light as an alert to an incoming call, so unless he is sat with it, he won't know I am ringing. I need to alert Josh that Cain may know their location now. The Kingston phone lines have a block to stop anyone tapping into them, but if you're a skilled IT fanatic which I am told Cain is, he can probably break through it. I will wait until our scheduled call tomorrow and if there is no answer, I will have no choice but to go to them.

The next day we walk along the beach, it's not warm but it isn't too cold. We are wrapped up in our coats and its quite pleasant as the wind blows in our face and hair. We walk hand in hand not speaking just taking in the world around us. Bella is so happy. This is something we need to do more often. Take a break from the busy city life. I want this life for my family, relaxed and carefree.

I'm not sure how long this bubble will last it could be days or weeks but I know the end is near.

It's just gone midnight. Bella and I are in bed, my phone buzzes lighting up the room with an incoming call. I look at the screen to see Mr Graves's name flashing at me. I quickly but quietly leave the room.

"Yes?"

Chapter 19

Damien

"I've had word on Cains where abouts. He knows where they are. He's probably there already. I am on my way, about 20 minutes away."

"No Mr Graves leave this to me do not go near them."

"I have to, If I explain to Cain, it may defuse the situation."

I have no idea how this will pan out. I just know I need to get myself and my team there as soon as possible.

"I am 30 minutes away. Ring me when you get there and let me know the situation."

I end the call and take a moment to mentally prepare myself. This is the moment I have been waiting for. The time I knew would arrive. The time to end Cain once and for all. I am ready.

"Sweetheart, you need to get dressed. We need to leave quickly."

"Why what's going on?"

"We are going to Josh and Chloe. They need our help."

Bella's eyes widen, she immediately climbs out of bed. Quickly throwing on her tracksuit we are out of the cottage and speeding down the motorway in seconds.

We have been staying 30 minutes away from Josh and Chloe. I also have members of my team in various locations nearby. They didn't know they were placed there for that reason, just that they were completing a mission. They will be arriving about the same time we will. Bella will stay with them while I sort Cain, once and for all.

Bella is staring out of the window, twiddling her fingers.

"Everything will be ok. This is the end of it all now. I promise."

The 30 minutes seem to take longer, but thankfully the roads are clear and we reach their location minutes earlier than planned. I stop on the road just out of view of the beach cottage Josh and Chloe are staying in. Mike and Frank pull in behind me. There is a car parked at the back which I recognise as Mr Graves.

"Come with me." I open Bella's door, take her hand and lead her to Frank and Mike's car.

"You stay here with the guys until I come back." Mike gets out of the car to speak to me.

"Whatever happens you do not leave her, understand? Both of you by her side until I return. If anything should happen, you drive none stop and take her to her parents."

More of the team arrive and base themselves around the cottage.

"Nobody enter until I say so." Everything seems

very quiet. Too quiet. Eery.

I can hear the sea crashing against the shore in the distance, but other than that, not a sound.

The whole area is in darkness, the sea looks black with only the reflection of the moon making the waves visible. The cottage is dark apart from a light coming through the curtains in the downstairs front window.

With my gun in my hand, I make my way over to the cottage. The security system was switched off an hour ago. That will be Cains doing. My stride is quick and long. Across the soft sand my footsteps hardly make a sound. I creep up the front porch steps as silently as I can. I peer through the slight gap in the curtains.

SH*T I see Josh on the floor. I see Cain and Graves arguing. I quickly assess the situation. If I go in this way they'll see me straight away. I make my way around to the back as quietly as I can until……

I hear a gun shot. I run to the back of the cottage. I race up to the door with my gun in front of me ready to fire.

The back door is open. I'm quiet as I enter the living area. I hear Cain shouting. I follow the sound of his voice to the front of the cottage. I see the back of his head. Without a second thought, I aim at his skull and pull the trigger.

BOOM

Cain stays standing for a second or two and I think I may need to shoot him again. But he eventually falls like the dead weight he is. As he lands on the floor I am met with the eyes of a tortured, broken looking Chloe. Horror fills me. I look to my left and see Josh. He is lying in an incredibly worrying amount of blood.

I go and sit beside my best friend.

The cottage fills with King security followed by the paramedics.

"Come on Josh. You're stronger than this. Invincible me and you. I can't do it without you." I squeeze his shoulder and reluctantly leave him to let the paramedics do their job.

Cain is gone, good riddance, the paramedics have covered him with a sheet. Graves looks like he's hanging in there, I couldn't care less either way. The Police have arrived. I go outside to speak to them. But not before I go to the car and check on my Bella. The car door opens as I walk towards it, Bella jumps into my arms. "You're ok, thank goodness you're ok!" I squeeze her as tight as I can. I need to feel her warmth.

"Yes. I'm ok. It's over. The gunman after Chloe is dead."

"Is Chloe ok?"

"She's going to need you sweetheart. She's been through a lot. When Chloe's taken in the ambulance you follow behind with Frank and Mike. You stay at the hospital with Chloe, and I will meet you there later on."

"Ok. And Josh is he ok?"

"He's not in a good way. The paramedics are with him. I need to get back over there. I will see you soon. I love you."

"I love you too."

I speak to the police, give them my statement and refer them to one of my team who will fill them in on the rest. My stomach is in knots, my heart is breaking. My best friend cannot leave me, I will not let it happen. When I enter the cottage again Graves is being covered with a sheet. I feel nothing for the man. Only that I wish he hadn't been born or hadn't fathered an evil waste of a human being.

"I'm sorry sir, he's gone." I look to see a paramedic looking sympathetically at me. He must be mistaking my stare at My Graves for concern.

"Good riddance," I say before I turn to look for my best friend. I see Josh surrounded by the critical care team. He is coved in wires, his face and mouth are filled with tubes.

"How's he doing?" I nod towards Josh, the paramedic's eyes follow my line of sight.

"He's in a bad way. But he's in the best hands."

Bella

I watch Chloe being wheeled out of the cottage into an ambulance. My heart breaks, I almost don't recognise her. Frank pulls our car out and follows closely behind to the hospital.

Chloe is settled in a private room when I'm finally allowed to see her.

"You can go in now but she's sleeping." I thank the nurse and sit by Chloe's bedside.

"Hey Chloe. It's Bella, it's so good to see you. The

doctors will have you fixed up in no time, you'll soon be home with us." I whisper as I take her hand in mine. I know she isn't asleep I can tell by her breathing, I've known her long enough. But for whatever reason Chloe doesn't want to speak right now and that is fine. But I will make sure she knows that I am here.

"I'm going to take good care of you. I have so much to tell you. I've missed you so much."

I kiss her hand rest my head on the side of the bed as I have a silent cry. What we've been through these past 2 years is unbelievable. I should write a book. Surely things can only get better from here.

I drift off to sleep praying for a brighter future for us all.

When I wake Chloe is still holding my hand, but she is definitely asleep now. She is doing her tell-tale sniffling snore that she does. I hear a tapping noise and turn to see Damien's face at the window of the door. I gently take my hand out of Chloe's grip and leave the room.

Damien looks pained. His stern facial expressions usually soften in my presence, but right now they remain, he looks overcome with worry. I wrap my arms around him, I nuzzle my face in his chest. He rests his chin on top of my head and takes a deep breath. We stay like this for a minute until I stand tall, being brave for the both of us "Let's go and get a coffee." Damien nods, with our arms still wrapped firmly around each other we make our way to the hospital café.

We find a table in a quiet corner and sit and drink our coffee.

"Come on, tell me how Josh is." I ask apprehensively, praying for good news.

"He's in surgery. Doctor said it would take about 6 hours." Damien rubs his face with his hands.

"How's Chloe doing?"

"She's been out of it the whole time I've been here. I'm going to try and speak to one of the doctors when we get back." We sit in silence for a few minutes.

"He's going to be ok Damien. You need to keep positive. Josh is strong like you, he won't let this take him, I'm sure of it." He stares into his coffee for a few moments before lifting his head to look at me.

"I really hope you're right, he's in a bad way."

"The doctors will fix him up good as new." I'm not sure if its something to do with the pregnancy or the fact that I have no choice, but my only thoughts are positive and strong ones. We will all get through this, we have to, the alternative does not bear thinking about.

When I think I have helped Damien feel a little better, we return to Chloe's room. Her eyes are closed and she is very still. It must be the medication making her sleepy. She hasn't opened her eyes since I've been here. I sit by her bedside and hold her hand. I try to ignore the bruising and swelling which has started to appear on her face, it looks so sore and swollen. Her head is wrapped in bandages as well as one of her ears. She would not be impressed if she could see herself now. Chloe always likes to look her best, especially around handsome doctors. Not that I have noticed, none of them are a patch on my husband.

Even though she is asleep, I talk to her about our childhood. Reminiscing about all the memories we made. We were inseparable from the moment we met in nursery. Chloe was always that bit bigger and stronger than me. We were like two opposites that just attracted instantly. In primary school she used to steal the best bits of my lunch, then boss me about in the playground, but she was always there to protect me. If anyone dare come near me or not let me win in a game, she would pull their hair out. Most weekends Chloe would stay at my house, Chloe's grandma was quite old fashioned, she didn't have sky TV or a computer, so Chloe came and used ours. My mum and dad loved her like their own, they still do. Damien is sat in the corner of the room laughing at the stories of our teenage years, how we used to sneak alcohol from her grandma's drinks cabinet. We would pour a little bit out of each one so she wouldn't notice. We would mix them all together in a 2 litre bottle of coke and sit in the park around the corner and drink it. I shudder thinking about it, vodka, whiskey, sherry, rum and goodness knows what else all mixed together, yuck. Then there were parties neither of us were allowed to go to so I would tell my mum and dad I was staying at hers and she would say she was staying mine. It worked a treat until Chloe's cat died and her grandma turned up at my house early in the morning. Dam cat. We were grounded for months.

"I hope our baby isn't as crafty as you two."

"They won't be able to get away with anything with you as their dad. You'll have them micro chipped at birth! They'll be fitted with some safety device that tells you where they are at all times and doesn't let them wander more than a metre away from you, poor thing."

"That's not a bad idea." I can see Damien's brain working.

"I was joking. Oh, Chloe I am really going to need your help in preventing Damien from making my child's life boring as hell." After a good giggle about our past I start to yawn, my adrenaline is definitely starting to wear off.

Damien gets me a blanket and some pillows and I snuggle up on the chair next to Chloe.

"My Bella's need to rest. I'll keep an eye on you, just relax." With a rub on my tummy and a kiss to my head, Damien dims the lights and leaves the room. Exhausted, I am soon asleep.

I wake to sound of alarms, doctors and nurses flood the room and surround Chloe. Damien lifts me out of the chair and quickly carries me out into the hallway.

Chapter 20

Chloe

My heart is broken and physically hurts. I don't want to live anymore. The love of my life is dead. Why didn't I realise sooner how strong my feelings were for Josh, I should have told him, now he will never know.

We could have had a wonderful life together. I wish I had died in that shooting at the youth centre so that Josh would have lived. He was a wonderful man. The kindest man I had ever met.

All I brought him was pain. He deserved so much more.

Bella has been with me since I arrived, but I can't bring myself to talk to her. I have pretended to be asleep. She has talked none stop trying to comfort me. I have listened to her talk about our childhood, our nursery years right through to our adult. We had some great times. I have always looked out for her. But Bella no longer needs me. She has Damien, and with a new baby, she will be just fine without me. If only I had died too.

Once I am left alone, I will end the pain. I want to be with my love once again.

I hope he forgives me. I'm sure he will.

Bella finally stops chatting and falls asleep. I quickly take my opportunity.

I pull the canular out of my hand and use the sharpness of the needle to stab into the vein in my wrist. It goes in easily. The skin is very thin on the inside of my wrists, I can clearly see the blue of the vein running down my arm. I trace the vein with the needle. It's tougher than it was going in, I have to press a little harder, but I manage easily enough. It's less painful than I imagine.

Blood pours as it pumps out of the vein and spills onto the white bedding. It comes out quicker than I expect. The next wrist is harder to do as my hand is covered in blood. It is warm and sticky, it makes me lose my grip on the needle. After a few tries, I manage it. That wrist also spills as my heart pumps. I lay back and think about my life. I think about my mother and how she must have met Mr Graves. How long had she known him? Did she love him? So many questions I will never get answers to. Having a father like him I suppose it was inevitable trouble would find me eventually.

I can feel the bed getting wetter around me. I start to feel lightheaded. I close my eyes, relaxing, waiting to drift off into that deep sleep you can never be awoken from. I start to see bright colours and lights. It's like when you stare at the sun for too long and your vision is like a kaleidoscope.

My body feels lighter. I enjoy the peace and release, but that is soon disturbed.

I hear loud noises.

Oh no.

I hear the sound of hospital alarms. I look down and see wires taped to my chest. I forgot to remove the heart monitor. The door bursts open with nurses who gasp at the sight of me. One of them bangs a button on the wall which sets off even more alarms. The nurses rush over to me and wrap my wrists in sheets. Holding my arms above my head they shout to other medics who enter the room. I close my eyes and let the tiredness take me away, hoping I have done enough, praying they didn't get to me in time.

Hours later I wake up.

Well, it feels like hours. The blinds are open on the window and the sun streams in. I look down at myself. I am in a clean white bed and my wrists are bandaged. I've a new canular, a heart monitor along with a drip and a bag of blood hanging at the side of me. In the corner of the room sits a Kings security guard. He's not one I recognise but he looks at me with sympathy.

"Hello Chole. I'm Frank. How are you feeling?"

I put my head back down, close my eyes and face the opposite direction.

Seriously, I can't do anything right. Everyone will be watching me like a hawk now. Well done Chloe, you moron.

Minutes later Bella and Damien enter the room. Frank has obviously informed them I am awake. I stay still with my eyes closed.

"Chloe!" Bella throws her arms around me. She sobs into my neck.

"Talk to me Chloe, please." I feel terrible for upsetting her like this but I just can't bear the hurt on her face.

"Leave her to rest Bella. You stay here with Frank, I'm going to check on Josh."

Wait?

What?

Did he just say Josh?

I sit blot up right in bed.

"Josh is alive?!" Damien stops on his way out of the door and turns towards me.

"Yes, by some miracle yes, he is Chloe. And he will be needing you to help him get better. So you better sort yourself out and be ready for when he wakes up!" He then turns and walks through the door. I can't believe it. I look at Bella who looks heartbroken.

"It's true? Tell me it's true Bella. Is Josh alive?"

"Yes Chloe. He's in bad shape and the doctor says he has a long road of recovery ahead of him, but he won't be dying anytime soon. He is definitely alive."

My heart bursts with emotion. My chest constricts. I can hardly breathe.

Tears stream from my eyes. I hear a wailing noise around me and realise that the sound is coming from me. Bella sits on my bed and pulls me into her. Holding me tight she rocks me and mutters words I can't make out. I'm in utter shock. I am overwhelmed.

I stay in Bella's arms while my brain begins to refunction.

"I need to see him."

"You will soon, but you need to get better first."

"No, I need to see him now." I look around and find the nurses call button, I press it multiple times until a nurse arrives.

"I need to go see my boyfriend."

"I don't advise that just yet Chloe, we have only just got you stable. You lost a lot of blood."

"I don't care. I take full responsibility if anything happens to me. If you don't remove these tubes from me right now, I will remove them myself." The nurse looks displeased with my request but starts to remove the heart monitor. She knows I mean business.

"We can get you in a wheelchair and you can take your drips with you. I'll call for a porter now so we can get you on your way." I am not happy about being in a wheelchair, but I do feel rather dizzy so its probably best to do as the nurse says.

I am wheeled into a room which is dimly lit. There are lots of machines in here, each making different beeping noises with flashing lights.

There's a bed in the middle of the room. In it lies my Josh.

My heart tightens. I honestly thought I'd never see

him again. I thought I had lost him forever.

He's lying slightly upright. His shoulders and arms are bare, but his chest is wrapped in bandages. He looks comfortable and peaceful. Damien is seated at the side of him but stands when we enter.

"I'll give you some time together." I wait while Damien and the porter leave the room. When we are alone I wheel myself to his side.

"I'm so sorry Josh. I'm so sorry I brought this to you. I should leave you, it's my fault you're in here. But I can't. I am too selfish. I cannot live without you Josh. I didn't realise how empty I was before I met you. You make me feel full. Complete." I take hold of his hand, he gives me a little squeeze. I squeeze him back.

"I love you Josh." His head turns towards me. His eyelids flutter open.

Our eyes lock.

His stare fills me with strength. Although he doesn't say a word, in that moment, I know he will be ok.

We will be ok.

Josh

I open my eyes still half asleep. Although the room is dark, I recognise the familiar layout of my teenage bedroom. The football trophies on the shelf above my desk, my cricket bat lent up against the wall, the humming sound of the filter in the fish tank next to my bed. Its then I hear it, the sound that woke me. Angry, raised voices. Male voices. I quietly get out of bed and open my door a crack to listen. I hear my dad, he's asking whoever it is to leave. The other male shouts back at him, refusing. I can't quite make out their conversation, but I can hear the distress in my dad's voice. Anger and adrenaline build inside me. I swing open my door and make my way across the landing to the stairs. As I reach the top, I hear the sound that haunts my nights. The whip like crack surrounded by a boom that you feel in every microorganism in your body. The sound of a gunshot. I make my way downstairs two steps at a time. Bursting into the kitchen I find my dad lying on the floor. In the corner of my eye, I see a man leave through the back door. But unlike the other thousands of times I have relived this nightmare, I follow him. I make my way out into the back garden and find him stood with his back to me. I then feel the cold heavy metal in my hand. I look down to see a handgun. Without a second thought I aim at the man's head and pull the trigger. A dark red spot in the back of his head grows larger as he drops to the floor. After finally ending the man who took my dad away from me, I need to see his face. To look in his eyes. I push him with my foot to roll him over, but as I do, I'm pulled back into darkness. I am no longer standing in my back garden; I am lying down. I force my eyes open, and I see it.

I see the end of my nightmares. I see Chloe.

Chapter 21

Chloe

The weeks and months that follow are hard and wonderful all at the same time. There's pain, pain for Josh in his recovery, pain for me watching him struggle in frustration, And love, so much love. They say you can't have one without the other, there's no pain without love and no love without pain. One of the universes great challenges and I am grateful for it every day.

Josh and I are living with Bella and Damien. Josh has had two serious lifesaving operations, one to repair damage the bullets did to his organs and another to remove a bullet. They had to leave one of them in as it was too dangerous to remove. There's been lots of physio and physical treatment for Josh and he has pushed himself to the limit. He's thankfully back to his fit self, apart from a few scars and some aches and pains now and again, which I'm sure he over exaggerates for attention, he's good as new. It has been difficult to get our heads around what we have all been through. It is, however, undeniable that we were all destined to meet. This was the universes way of bringing us all together. A little harsh, If you ask me but it worked out all the same.

It turns out that Cain, Mr Graves son was the one who murdered Josh's Dad. When Josh was a teenager, his dad got himself in a lot of debt. He had lost his job and things had spiralled out of control. He hadn't wanted to worry Josh's Mother, so he had borrowed some money off a loan shark. That loan shark being Mr Graves, my biological father. At that time Cain was the debt collector. Josh's father had known they were loan sharks but hadn't thought there was much risk, as he was waiting for a business deal to come through. He knew he would be able to pay it back with the large interest rate.

When the time came to collect payment, rather than meeting at the arranged place, Cain had turned up at Josh's house. Even though Josh's dad made the payment in full and on time, Cain murdered him anyway. Josh unfortunately walked in on this horrendous scene leaving him with heart breaking nightmares. This incident however led to him to specialise in intensive defence and protective training. He then set up 'King security' with Damien. So regardless of how intensely heart breaking our past has been, we must respect it, and understand that it is the universes way of directing us to our destiny.

I'm lying in bed next to Josh. He's on his back with one hand under his head and the other around me. I have my head on his chest listening to him snoring lightly.

"JOSH!" Damien's voice bellows through the house. Josh jumps up out of bed and is out of the door in a second. I quickly get up, put on my dressing gown and follow him out on to the landing. I find him in Damien and Bella's room.

"I'll get the car, meet you down there." Josh says as he kisses me on the head and runs down the stairs. Bella's is sat on the bed being sick in a bowl.

"Hey Bella, what's going on? Are you ok?" I sit next to her and rub her back while Damien starts throwing stuff in a suitcase.

"She's been being sick for half an hour now, she has pains in her stomach which aren't going away. I rang the hospital and they said to bring her in right away."

"Damien, calm down what are you doing?" Bella questions as he rummages through their wardrobes.

"I'm trying to find the baby's things, and what do you need?!"

"Damien, Bella's hospital bag and the baby's bag have been packed for weeks. They are in the nursery ready to go, just sit down a sec and take a breath. Now Bella, tell me, how do you feel?"

"I just feel sick, and I have this pain in my stomach, but it could just be the fact that I'm heaving so much. It doesn't feel like a contraction. It's probably just something I have eaten."

"It could be, you are 3 weeks early, but as baby is breach, it's best to get you checked out. Ok I'll grab some plastic bags and some wipes in case you're sick on the way and I'll get your bags from the nursery. Damien, you help Bella down to the car, I'll meet you there."

When we get to the hospital the doctors are waiting for us. Damien carries Bella in and puts her on the bed. His protective alpha male coming out in full force. Bella is hooked up to different machines making beep noises and coloured tapes are put around her stomach. The doctor examines Bella and confirms the baby is still breach.

"I think it is safest for mother and baby to deliver now. Please don't panic, but in a moment I will sound an alarm and a number of my medical team will enter the room. We will be doing an emergency section. Protocol states we need to have baby here within 20 minutes of the alarm. Only Dad can be in the operating theatre, but you both can wait in the family room." The doctor nods to myself and Josh as she presses a red button on the wall. Bright lights fill the room, and an extremely high pitch alarm fills our ears. Doctors and nurses wearing scrubs burst into the room and surround Bella. Don't panic she said, Ha, no chance of that. I look at Damien as Josh and I leave the room. He looks white as a sheep and completely overwhelmed. I make a silent prayer for them to be ok.

Josh gets us a coffee and we sit on the leather sofa in the family room.

We then hear loud footsteps in the hall outside the door. We both go to investigate. Its Damien in full scrubs wandering up and down with his hands on his head.

"Damien what's going on?" Josh grabs his arms.

"They told me to get these scrubs on and then go to the operating theatre, but I don't know where it is?" Josh holds his shoulders and guides him down the hall to doors which have a sign above saying 'Operating theatre' he knocks on and the double doors open immediately.

Bella

This is it, this is where I am going to lose my baby. I am so scared. Not for me, I really don't care what happens to me anymore, it's all about my child. When that alarm sounded, and all those doctors and nurses entered the room I knew things weren't right. I just hope my baby is strong and these doctors can work a miracle, because that's what my baby deserves.

I sit as still as I can while the epidural is inserted into my back. Once it's in I lie on the bed and a sheet is hung at my waist so I can't see what is happening down there. There's a nice nurse at the side of me explaining what is going on, reassuring me everything is fine, but I don't really believe him. An oxygen mask is placed over my face, I start to panic, the nurse sees this and asks me if I'm ok.

"I'm scared I'm going to be sick again." Oh no what would happen then, if I was sick while my stomach was cut open?

"Don't worry we have given you an anti-sickness drug, so you won't be." Ok that makes me feel a bit better. Then I realise Damien still isn't here. But as I look up, he walks through the door in full scrubs with a 'deer caught in the headlights' look on his face. He sits at the side of my head and takes my hand. It is shaking uncontrollably.

"Is she ok? Why is she shaking?" Damien demands to the nurse at the side of me.

"It's a mixture of the drugs and her adrenaline. Perfectly normal."

"Ready?!" The doctor at the end of my bed asks the room. I can't see her, but I know she's there, along with a number of other people.

"They're going to begin now." I nod to the kind nurse.

"Argh!" I scream in pain. Damien stands in fury.

"Could you feel that?" The nurse asks concerned. I nod.

"It's ok, sometimes the epidural takes a little longer to work. Here, have some gas and air. We will try again in 2 minutes. Just to make you aware though, if you can still feel it after the 2 minutes we will have to put you to sleep, and then your husband won't be able to be here for the birth."

I can't take that away from him, plus I need to be awake to make sure my baby is ok.

The nurse signals to me that the 2 minutes is over, I brace myself for the pain. I feel the knife enter my skin, the tissue and muscle's part. It's not as intense as before. I can handle it. I smile at the nurse to say I am fine, although I am not sure he believes me. The longer it goes on the less I feel. I feel movement in my stomach but not pain. I watch the clock as the doctor said the baby needed to be born in 20 minutes. We came in the theatre at 2:00am its now 2:20. Damien is still holding my hand and staring at me intently. I can't look at him. He's making my worry more. At 2:22 there's a commotion and I hear the doctor say

"She's here, it's a little girl." She's held up over the sheet for a second and then whisked away. I look at Damien and we both smile and sob in relief.

That relief and smile soon disappears from our face when we realise we haven't heard a cry. You know that when a baby is born the first thing they do is cry, unless there is something wrong.

Damien kisses my hand and then stands to see where our girl has gone.

"She's ok, sir, they're just helping her clear her airways and giving her a little oxygen, perfectly normal in c section deliveries. Damien sits and nods, taking my hand again. After what feels like hours, we finally hear the noise we have been waiting for. My heart grows.

"Dad, would you like to come and cut the cord?"
Damien beams and stands, still holding my hand, reluctant to leave me.
"You go, look after our girl."
Feeling a little more relaxed now I lie and listen to

Damien talk to our little girl. It's the most amazing sound I have ever heard in my life. He speaks softly, telling her how beautiful she is, how much he already loves her, and how he will protect her always. He's going to be a wonderful father, he already is. She's a lucky girl.

"Let's go and see your mummy."

Damien returns to the side of me with our little girl wrapped in a fluffy white towel. She's crying, but when I start to speak, she stops and opens her eyes a little.

"She recognises her mummy's voice." Damien puts her beside my head so I can kiss her. She smells incredible. She smells like my baby, a smell I have never smelt before but that I instantly recognise as *my* baby's smell.

"Does she have a name?"

"Daisy." We both say together.

When Damien proposed, which was also the time I told Damien I was pregnant, we were in a field of Daisies. We spent hours in that field making daisy chains and planning our future together. It's one of my most treasured memories of us together. We get settled in the recovery room, Daisy is on my chest fast asleep, I can't take my eyes off her. Damien can't take his eyes off the both of us, that is until Chloe and Josh burst through the door.

"Aaahh my baby niece, let me see, let me see." Chloe dives over to us pushing Damien out of the way so she can get closer.

"Daisy, meet your Aunty Chloe and Uncle Josh."

"She's just like you Bella."

"Congratulations mate." Damien and Josh hug in their usual manly way where they slap each others back. That is until Damien surprisingly grabs and holds Josh, squeezing him tight. I smile at the sight. Chloe sees it too and looks at me with tears in her eyes.

We are family and we are so lucky to have each other.

Chapter 22

6 Months later
Josh

I am sat on a sun lounger by the pool in Sorrento, Italy. We are here for the wedding of Damien and Bella. They are of course already married. But nobody other than Chloe and I know that. Bella always wanted a big wedding, and Damien wants Bella to have want she has dreamed of. Damien is actually half Italian on his dad's side. He has family over here, aunts, uncles and so on. Seeing as Damien's parents aren't able be here in body, Bella thought being in Italy, the place where his parents met and married would compensate a little for that. I think she made a very good choice. It is a beautiful place. Today is the wedding day. It is actually Damien and Bella's first anniversary. They planned it that way so that they would always be able to celebrate their anniversary on its original day. I am sat in the shade watching Clo chatting away to Bella's family. She's such a magnet. So friendly and kind, her personality is infectious, people just want to be around her.

I spot two guys at the bar talking about her while making provocative faces towards her. Not that she notices. I stand by my sunbed preparing to go over there if Chloe needs me. Jealousy runs through me. I try to think of an excuse to get her back in our room and have her all to myself. A waiter carrying a silver tray approaches me.

"You like anything to drink signore?" I ignore him not taking my eyes off Chloe and the two morons at the bar. "Ahh, I see, she's a very beautiful lady." Following my line of sight, he too begins to stare at Chloe. "Very nice…. How you say?…. Boobies?" I turn and stare at the teenage looking waiter. Is Italy full of imbeciles? My face is angry, and I see the terror appear on his face when I look at him. He steps back away from me, so I take a step towards him. He takes another step back but cannot go any further as his heel rests on the edge of the pool. I close the gap between us.

"For your information, no, we do not say 'boobies' unless you are 5 years old, and that beautiful lady over there, is mine." I give him a shove to the shoulder.

He falls backwards into the pool. The splash and wail from the waiter as he enters the pool draws everyone's attention to us. At first people almost go to help him, but after seeing me walking away from the scene people continue with whatever they are doing. The waiter soon gets pulled out by his manager who shouts something in Italian at him.

"Did you just push that poor boy in the pool?" Chloe glares at me with her hands on her hips.

"Me? Nooooo, he just tripped and fell in."

"Ha, yeah, why don't I believe you."

"You're needed upstairs. Some, maid of honour chief bridesmaid thing?"

"Oh ok." Chloe turns to the guests she's been taking to. "Sorry guys need to go. I'll see you at the wedding." Well, that was easier than I thought. I should have used this excuse ages ago.

We get out of the lift and Chloe turns left to go to the bridal suit.

"No not that way, you are needed in our room."

"Our room?" she questions confused but happily follows me to our suite. I let Chloe in first and she realises as soon as I have shut the door that I have got her here under false pretences. A smirk soon appears across her beautiful face.

"You know you could have just told me it was you who needed me up here. I would have been just as eager, if not a little more actually."

"Oh really?"

"Yes really." Chloe pulls the pathetic excuse for a sundress over her head and unties her bikini top, with one pull of a cord it drops to the floor. After a week in the sun Chloe's skin is even more delicious. I close the gap between us, my mouth hungrily claims her as mine. I throw her over my shoulder and carry her into the bedroom. I playfully throw her on the bed and remove my vest and shorts. This woman makes me feel like I will pass out if I don't have her, she is the oxygen to my lungs, the blood to my heart. I take her in my arms and fill her with as much passion and love as I can. I hope she can feel what she does to me. Chloe wraps herself around me, my heart swells as it always does when she makes her sounds of appreciation. Hungrily kissing and sucking my skin I know she feels as strongly as I do. Our bodies work in unison as if they were made perfectly to fit each other.

"Over here." Chloe moves over to a sofa in the corner of the room, with one leg up on the sofa seat and her hands on the arm of the chair she opens up widely for me. I take a second to admire the view.

"Come on stud we've not got all day!" Chloe likes to have me in all sorts of positions, which is fine by me. My spicy little minx. I take her on the sofa, then over the dressing table.

Once we've recovered in the bedroom we start again in the bathroom. Once on the sink, then in the shower, and finish up in the bathtub.

"I love you, you know."

"I know, but I love you more Clo." I tickle her feet which makes her wriggle splashing water over the edge on the bath.

"Do you think we will get married one day?"

"Most definitely." I answer. I hope she feels the same about marriage because I will be asking her very soon. She smiles and stands.

"Come on big boy. We've got a wedding to get ready for. People will be wondering where we are."

The wedding is at Santa Maria church in Positano. We are getting boats from the hotel around the island to the harbour by the church. After the service all 200 guests will board a super yacht. From there we will cruise around Italy late into the night, being waited on and entertained. Knowing Damien, it will be spectacular and something every one of the guests will remember forever.

I'm standing at the end of the aisle at the front of the church next to Damien. The guests are all seated waiting for the bride's arrival.
The large double doors open with a crack. Music begins and the guests turn, waiting in anticipation for their first glimpse of the bride.

Chloe
The doors to the church open and the music starts signalling the entrance of the bride. As soon as the instrumental starts, I fill with emotion. Its 'Kiss the girl' from the little mermaid, but this version melts your heart. It's being sung by an incredible male singer alongside a pianist, and a range of wood wind instruments. They chose this song because the Little Mermaid is Daisy's favourite movie. I think it is perfect, the first two verses sound like they were written for Damien and Bella.

"There you see her
Sitting there across the way
She don't got a lot to say
But there's something about her
And you don't know why
But you're dying to try
You wanna kiss the girl

Yes, you want her
Look at her, you know you do
Possible she wants you too
There is one way to ask her
It don't take a word
Not a single word
Go on and kiss the girl"

Damien knew from the first moment he saw Bella that there was something about her, he knew she was the one and has stopped at nothing to have and protect her. Watching them now is the most beautiful experience. The love in Damien eyes as he watches her walk down the aisle is incredible.

Bella walks in front of me being held steady by her Dad. Katie walks behind me and Tiff behind her. Baby Daisy the flower girl has already been carried down the aisle by her grandma, Bella's Mum. All the flowers are daisies, of course, the bouquets, the entrance door flowers, and the end of aisle flowers. All different sizes but all white with yellow centres. Our bridesmaid dresses are very pale-yellow silk. The wedding is the perfect complement to the beautiful white and gold interior of the church. The breath-taking aisle and arches of the church make me feel like I am in a fairy tale wedding.

It's a traditional catholic wedding and I am honoured to be part of it.

Damien and Bella beam at each other throughout the ceremony. Josh looks so proud as the best man.

He's so handsome too. I am truly lucky to have him. He catches me staring at him during one of the hymns, he gives me a sexy wink making my knees feel weak and my cheeks flush.

Once husband and wife are pronounced, we follow the happy couple out on the steps at the front of the church. The photographers take the traditional photos and passers-by stand and watch taking their own pictures. It is always a treat to see a bride and groom but Damien King in a wedding suit and Bella King in a wedding gown- that is a view of a lifetime.

We all board the super yacht.

"Oh. My. God! Josh how amazing is this I have never seen anything like it."

"Well, you know Damien, he doesn't do anything by halves."

The yacht is more like a cruise ship, once you're in you don't feel like you are on a boat.

We are greeted with champagne, cocktails, canapes and gift bags. The bags are filled with everything you could need. Suncream and glasses, perfume and make up, paracetamol and Rennies, you name it, it's in here. We are led through the yacht up to the top deck.

The view is incredible. Live music fills the air, the atmosphere is perfect. Josh gets stopped talking to someone from the security team, so I make my way around the deck. I stand in the corner for a while, people watching, sipping my champagne. Everyone is chatting happily getting to know one another. Damien has hold of Daisy and is proudly introducing her to family and friends. Bella is talking with her mum and dad, they look so proud. The guests all look beautiful and are clearly enjoying themselves.

I spot Josh in the opposite corner, he has his back to me. Even from the back he makes me melt. Those big strong shoulders filling out his tailor made suit. His thick thighs and bum, I am one lucky lady. After a moment of gratefully admiring, I notice him suddenly stiffen. Immediately I rush over to him. An Italian looking man is stood beside him.

"Which bridesmaid?" I hear Josh demand as I get closer. If stares could put holes in heads, this guy would have two right about now.

"Hey there, I've been looking for you." I say as I push my way in between the two of them. I don't want anything or anyone spoiling Bella's day. The Italian looking man's stern facial expression turns friendly as he turns to look at me.

"I was just asking this kind gentleman who the beautiful bridesmaid was standing over there in the corner." The man says in a strong Italian accent.

"Ahh that would Katie." I smile, "Would you like me to introduce you......... Mr?"

"No, thank you that won't be necessary. Enjoy your evening." The guy takes another look at Katie, but then leaves in the opposite direction.

"I don't like that guy."

"You don't like any guy apart from Damien."

"I don't trust him. Did you notice how he avoided telling you his name?" I hadn't noticed but I also don't think it's that big of a deal. Surely everyone here is on the guest list, it can't be that hard to find out.

"Look everything is fine, there's more security on this yacht than in the whole of Italy. We've been through metal detectors and body searches to get on here. Please just relax."

Josh takes me in his arms and squeezes me kissing the top of my head. I know he worries about me, and it's his job to be suspicious and detect danger, but I wish he would just relax for one day.

"Come on let's go get me drunk." I give him a wink, he knows what that means. I am a little more? let's say adventurous at 'bedtime' when I have had a few drinks.

Josh finally relaxes and we have the most memorable day and evening. All the guests are treated like royalty. The yacht is one big party, catering for everyone. There have been magicians and entertainers for the children, Music and singers, a casino and the most incredible food and drinks selection.

All the guests are gathered on the outside deck watching the sun set. Josh links his arm in mine and gives me a little pull.

"Come with me." I follow Josh through the guests and up a narrow staircase. It brings us out on to a small deck at the top of the yacht. The view is incredible, I stand looking over the railings, the sun setting creates sparkles across the ocean. I expect to feel Josh behind me, so when don't, I turn to see him kneeling behind me. I hadn't noticed when I came up, obviously distracted by the view, but the deck is full of twinkling candles.

"Clo" Josh clears his throat.

"Chloe Karen. Ever since I met you, you made me crazy. Crazy about you, crazy insane and crazy in love. I know that life without you would not be worth living. You are the oxygen to my lungs, the blood to heart. Please put me out of my misery and wear this ring, promise you will marry me and always be mine?"

The smile on my face must be the goofiest smile there ever was.

"I always have been yours Josh, from the minute I met you." I hold out my hand and Josh slides a platinum band with a blue diamond in the centre.

"Oh my goodness. Josh it's a blue diamond like the ones we saw in the shop with my grandma's broach."

"It's not 'like' it is. And here's the other two. I had the broken bracelet made into an engagement ring and earrings. Do you like them?"

"They're perfect. Thank you." I love them, the blue reminds me of Josh's eyes.

Josh stands and holds me. We look into each other's eyes for a moment before he kisses me with love and tenderness.

I feel like the luckiest woman in the universe.

Epilogue.
6 months later
Bella

It's a busy day in the salon today. We are booked up with clients as well as having London fashion week to prepare for. I love the excitement and atmosphere of this time of year. I feel extremely lucky to be doing a job I love. I only work part time in the salon now. Daisy and Damien will always be my priority but that doesn't mean I can't do what I enjoy as well.

Chloe and Josh are back from their travels this weekend. Chloe wouldn't miss one of my shows for fashion week. They've been travelling the world since Damien and I got married. Chloe had never been abroad before going to Italy, but since then has caught the travel bug. Josh keeps whisking her away and spoiling her like she deserves. I know they'll want to get married and start a family soon so they're making the most of it before they settle down.

At the end of the day, I'm in the staffroom when Katie comes in looking pale.

"Bella? Can I have a quick word please?" Katie is one of my best friends after Chloe. I'm sensing something that makes me uneasy.

"Of course, what's up?"

"I'm really sorry Bella, I don't like to do this and leave you in a mess, but I'm going away for a while. I'm not sure how long I'm going to be gone but it's something I need to do."

Katie has recently split from her boyfriend. Good riddance I say. He was a jerk; she is far too good for him.

"That's ok, Katie, don't worry about the salon, but are you alright? You know you can tell me anything, I'm here for you Katie." Tears fill her eyes, so I wrap my arms around her. "Hey come on. Tell me what's wrong?" wiping her tears away she takes a deep breath.

"I just need to get away that's all." I sense there's more to this story, but I don't push. It isn't surprising she wants a change of scenery after her breakup.

"When do you leave?"

"Tomorrow."

"So soon? Well at least tell me where you're going?"

"Italy."

The End

Or is it just the Beginning?

If you have enjoyed I've Found Her please read on for a teaser of the next in the 'Found' series.

He Found Me

Prologue

Katie

When you're a teenager you say all sort of things you don't mean. Especially where young love is concerned. You don't expect to be held responsible for those words years later.

When I was 16 my mum took me on holiday to Italy. While she was off busying herself with the Italian waiters half her age, I was left to my own devises. I didn't mind. I have always enjoyed my own company. But on those two weeks I was never alone, and I loved every minute of it.

On the first day I was walking around the hotel grounds and I heard a whistle. I turned to see a boy peeping through the fence. He waved me over and we began to talk. The boy was Italian and spoke little English but something about him fascinated me, we just clicked. His name was Leonardo, but I called him Leo. He was 16 like me. Every day he climbed over that fence to get into the hotel. We had to be careful no one saw him. He was always so worried about being caught. The hotel was quite posh and expensive. I think he was poor and thought he would get in trouble if he was caught.

We spent every minute we could together. Some nights we even fell asleep under the stars. My mum didn't notice whether I was in my bed or not. Leo was my first holiday romance, my first love, my first everything. My heart broke when I had to leave him and come home. We promised to write to each other every week, which we did for two years. That was until one day I came home from college to find mum and I had been evicted from our house. We couldn't even go in and collect our things. We had nothing. I moved in with my dad after that. The worse thing about it was that I lost all my letters from Leo. I couldn't remember his address, I had kept all the letters in a box under my bed along with my address book. I was devastated. A few years later when Facebook came about, I tried to search for him, but I couldn't remember his surname, so it was useless.

In our last letter to each other, we promised that if neither of us were married when we turned 30 we would be together and marry each other.

Today is my 30th birthday and I have just received an invitation to my own wedding!

JOY MULLETT

Printed by Amazon Italia Logistica S.r.l.
Torrazza Piemonte (TO), Italy

59756371R00125